The Stars Over Beale Street

The Stars Over Beale Street
A Riley Press Publication
Eagle, MI 48822
rileypress@yahoo.com

Stars photo by Eidy Bambang-Sunaryo on Unsplash

Editing by Genevieve Scholl and Judith Hudson

Have you read?

The House on Beale Street by Loraine J. Hudson

(*first in the Beale Street Series*)

Chapter One

It was the cold that drove us inside after a night of stargazing, shivering and stamping and blowing on our fingers to warm them. Duffy maneuvered the heavy telescope and tripod over the threshold, vainly attempting to navigate past my prone and snoring dog, whose large frame blocked the doorway.

"I got a great shot of Saturn," Duffy panted, lifting the tripod one direction and then the other, and backing outside again. "Marianne, can you move Rowdy? I don't want to hit the doorframe with this. I'm guessing Chuck wouldn't appreciate me returning his equipment all banged up."

I bent toward my dog who, as best I could tell, hadn't even bothered to open his eyes. "Rowdy, for Heaven's sake," I protested, and wrapped my arms around his warm, furry body, pulling him gently across the tile floor and out of the way.

There he lay, all 140 pounds of him, a giant black bear of a dog, dreaming doggy dreams, as undisturbed and unflappable as ever. I spied a small spot of drool and I rubbed it away with the toe of my boot, glancing quickly over at Duffy. Fortunately, he was still wrestling with the telescope and hadn't noticed. Duffy and Rowdy were fast friends, but Duffy wasn't a fan of Rowdy's drooling in the same way I was.

I put my hands on my hips and regarded my dog. "Good thing we aren't burglars," I said loudly, but Rowdy still didn't stir. Of course, he knew my friend Duffy and I and the telescope weren't burglars and, for my part, I knew he was capable of becoming a different dog altogether when someone was bent on mischief, particularly when said mischief was aimed at me. I gave him a quick pat. "Never mind," I whispered. "You sleep away if you want."

Then I went back outside to help stow the gear Duffy had borrowed to allow us a delightful evening of stargazing. Carefully steering past the screen door, we had gotten the heavy apparatus nearly inside when a sound made us straighten and stare at each other, wide-eyed.

"What in the world was that?" said Duffy.

Although I knew we were on the safe streets of tiny Burtonville, and it was a frigid winter night where no self-respecting ghost would be abroad, I felt the hair rise on the back of my neck. The sound had been very ghost-like, indeed. A high wail in the distance somewhere between a shriek and a moan that wavered and died to stillness in the thin winter air. We gazed at each other, but the sound didn't recur. Duffy glanced over his shoulder and I shivered.

"What was that?" he repeated.

"I have no idea!" I exclaimed. "An animal of some sort?"

Rowdy had raised his big head and was looking past us out the door. The fact that the sound had disturbed Rowdy-the-nearly-undisturbable was reason enough to be alarmed.

"It sounded more human to me," Duffy said. "Let's get this equipment in and then go take a look."

We resumed our careful efforts, and soon the telescope was sitting safely on the tripod in the corner of my living room.

"I've got to rub it down soon," said Duffy, "so moisture doesn't condense on it—"

He was interrupted by the sound of sirens, and we both jumped. We had heard more commotion in the last five minutes than I'd experienced in several months. My little town of Burtonville was—with the exception of a couple of notable events during the fall—about the quietest place imaginable, and just the way I liked it.

Duffy frowned and turned to look at me. "Let's go see what's going on."

"Okay," I said, although I had no particular desire to go back outside. The combination of the cold, the general creepiness of that weird sound, and now the shrieking of sirens, made staying inside with some popcorn and hot chocolate a far more attractive option.

I compromised by snapping Rowdy's leash onto his collar and taking him with us into the frosty night. He would need an evening walk anyway, I reasoned, and if there were ghosts or other miscreants abroad ... well ... Rowdy could be a formidable ally if he stayed awake. We strolled to the end of the block and turned the corner, and the sirens stopped abruptly.

"I see lights out at the edge of town," Duffy commented. "Looks like maybe a fire."

I gazed past him at the flashing lights of emergency vehicles. "Oh no, I hope it's nothing serious. I'll call Ashley in the morning. She'll know."

Duffy grinned. "Of course, she will."

I punched his arm. "Her husband's on the volunteer fire department!"

Duffy just kept grinning. With the wails of the fire engine gone, the night had grown quiet again, and Duffy and I shuffled along the snowy sidewalk in companionable silence. The peculiar sound we had heard earlier did not return, to my relief.

Rowdy padded along next to me, sniffing here and there and lifting his leg on a snowbank. I kicked some loose snow over the spot, and we three turned to head back. My little house, nestled in the maples on quiet Beale Street, was calling me like a beacon. A cup of hot chocolate, a few minutes of reading and I would be all done for the night. I could feel my eyes getting heavy just thinking about it. That noise had probably been nothing. Maybe a cat defending its territory. I hoped it had a warm place to spend the night. And the sirens—perhaps it had been a false alarm.

Arriving at the house, Duffy held the door open for me, took off his coat and gloves and began flipping through his cell phone pictures. “Check out this shot!” he said. “That phone photo mount on the ‘scope is genius.”

I nodded. “Very nice. You can see the rings of Saturn perfectly! Make sure you tell Chuck thanks from me. He was really kind to loan us his gear. I’ll buy him a bottle of wine.”

“Good idea,” said Duffy. “Okay if I leave all the equipment in your living room ‘til I can come back and get it on the weekend?”

“If Chuck doesn’t care.”

“He won’t. He’s actually in Chile at the moment, up on a mountain at one of the big research telescope sites. He’ll be back in-country in a couple of weeks.”

“Ah,” I said, and because even though it probably *was* nothing, I couldn’t seem to let it go, I added, “So what do *you* think that sound was?”

“I think you were right that it was an animal. Maybe a raccoon?”

“Are raccoons normally out during the really cold winter nights? I thought they hibernated or went into a deep sleep or something.”

“A coyote?”

“Maybe,” I answered doubtfully. I walked to the window and looked out over the quiet town. The sound had been unnerving in a way I couldn’t quite identify, but the fact that it hadn’t returned, and that Rowdy was now back in his somnolent doggy world, interested only in having his night-time treat, was somewhat reassuring.

I complied with Rowdy's insistence on receiving the obligatory handful of bones while Duffy carefully wiped down the telescope and draped it with a lightweight cloth. He looked over his shoulder at me. "Not," he said, "that I worry about dog hair getting on Chuck's telescope. But just in case ..."

I smiled. Duffy was a good-looking man, smart, gentle and kind. And there were nights—like tonight—when I could imagine our relationship moving beyond friendship into a sweet and satisfying romance. I could want that. Perhaps I *did* want that, but not yet. Not now. If my dear friend Louise had been there, she would have remarked wryly that I'd been a widow for a decade, and how long did I intend to mourn Duane? Which would have made *me* tell Louise stubbornly that how ever long it had been, it was going to be a little bit longer, which was how all our conversations ended.

"I'll keep an eye on it," I said, nodding at the telescope. "Rowdy's too polite to shed around Chuck's equipment."

"Good," said Duffy, his hazel eyes twinkling. He shrugged into his coat again and reached for his gloves. "I'll give you a call tomorrow."

"Hot chocolate for the road?" I asked.

"Not tonight," Duffy said. "Work tomorrow and all that. Lucky you!"

"Right," I grinned. "No work for me. Lady of leisure."

He reached out a hand and set it gently on my hair—the closest thing he ever came to an embrace. He knew and understood about my husband, Duane, lost to a bullet in Afghanistan. What was more, Duffy and I had recently had a serious misunderstanding from which we had largely recovered, but not totally. His behavior toward me since that time had had a slightly tentative aspect that I regretted but which was unsurprising.

"Did you want to hit a movie Saturday?" I asked, and his hand dropped back to his side.

"Sure," he answered. "See if Louise wants to come."

"I'll ask her," I said.

Soon he had folded his tall frame into his car and backed down the drive, and I watched his taillights heading down Beale Street, turning right for the trip back to Peoria. I sighed and turned to Rowdy.

Abandoning the notion of hot chocolate, I said, "Bedtime, my man," to Rowdy, who was already asleep again, and went to my room to change, checking the front door twice to make sure it was locked and the security latch was in place. I peeked out the picture window, but I couldn't see the lights from the emergency vehicles. They seemed to have gone as well.

My little home in Burtonville was cozy, warm and comforting against the cold, clear night. I had bought it on what might be called a crazy impulse, but it had turned out to be exactly the right move—a small, welcoming space where I could do anything and everything I wanted to decorate it, enjoy it, and make it wholly and completely mine. And Rowdy's, of course.

There had been that hiccup with Duffy, and some major unpleasantness surrounding a local robbery, but that was several months ago, and all had been smooth sailing since that time. I dug my reading glasses out of my bedside stand, cast a fond glance at my favorite photo of Duane and me and picked up my paperback to read myself to sleep. But somehow, even there under my thick comforter, and with Rowdy snoring at my bedroom door, I could still hear the faint echo of that eerie sound in my head, like a wordless sob.

Chapter Two

"Hello?" I said breathlessly, holding my cell phone to my ear.

It had rung three times while I searched through the house for it, tripping over Rowdy, throwing aside sofa cushions, and digging in all my pockets. The fact that it had rung, stopped, rung, stopped, and then begun ringing again made it unquestionably a call from my neighbor, Ashley Midden. She would know I was at home, partly because her house was within shouting distance of mine, and partly because Ashley was an expert on everything and everyone in Burtonville. Knowing whether someone had gone out to run an errand or left to take a walk would be child's play for her, and the notion of leaving one's cell phone behind incomprehensible.

"Hey! 'Bout time," came Ashley's piping voice on the other end of the line, and I smiled. Ashley was the first neighbor I'd met in Burtonville, and after the business with the robbery and her kids camping out in my basement got sorted out, we'd become fast friends. "Were you in the back forty?"

"Back forty." I snorted. "Not 'til spring! No, I was drying my hair and then trying to find my phone. Duffy and I were out looking at the stars last night, and I left it in the kitchen."

"Looking at the stars! Did you freeze?"

"A little," I answered. "But when it's cold, it's clear and easier to see good stuff through the telescope. We had some great views. And Duffy took some spectacular photos."

"What color did you do?" Ashley asked, in one of those quicksilver changes of subject that one always had to navigate when talking with her.

"Color ... Oh, you mean my hair? I didn't color it."

"I thought you were going to take out the gray."

I looked at myself in the mirror and ran my fingers through my short curls. "Nah," I said. "Guess not."

"How come? You'd be really hot."

"You don't think I'm hot now?"

There was a short silence on the other end of the phone and then Ashley burst out laughing. "Duffy thinks so."

"Never mind that," I said.

"Hey," said Ashley. "When do you want to come over and work on the wallpaper? I bought another roll, so I think there's enough to do my whole entryway now."

"Any day," I answered. "I'm free except Saturday."

"What about Sunday?" asked Ashley. "We could get together for a couple of hours and then go over to the Methodist church. We need to get there to hear about the project."

"What project?" I asked. I turned my head from side to side and gazed at my reflection in the mirror. Maybe I *should* color my hair. It was once a pretty walnut color, but now it was shot with silver at my temples. And maybe in a couple of other places, too, if I was honest with myself. I remembered Duane's and my wedding pictures. My hair had been longer then, and free of any gray. I sighed.

"We're putting together a quilt," Ashley went on. "Everyone's making a square, and embroidering it with a Burtonville landmark. It's going to be donated to the historical society. You know how to embroider, right?"

"Um." I turned resolutely away from the mirror. "I guess so. Sort of. By 'everyone,' what do you mean?"

Do I really know how to embroider? I wondered. I wasn't so sure. My grandmother taught me when I was in my teens, but embroidering hadn't exactly been on my agenda since then.

"They need something like a hundred squares. It's a big quilt," Ashley went on. "I'm supposed to be helping to recruit volunteers, and I already volunteered you."

I sighed. *Right. I could always look at some online videos,* I thought, and said, "I surrender. I can do one if someone gives me instructions. How about Louise? Could she help? I'm pretty sure she can embroider."

"Sure," answered Ashley. She yawned. "Wow, I'm tired. Matt got called to a fire last night and I had a hard time getting back to sleep. The trials of a volunteer firefighter's wife."

"What was on fire? We heard the sirens."

"Oh, it didn't turn out to be anything serious. Matt said it was easy to put out."

"How would something like that start in the middle of the night?"

"Weird, isn't it? Someone was burning trash. And trash can smolder a long time. People forget that. But Matt said ..." She trailed off.

"Matt said what?"

There was a long silence, then Ashley went on, "It'll probably turn out to be nothing. But that fire's being investigated as arson."

"Really? It was deliberate? The fire was set by someone deliberately?"

"They don't know. The family swore they hadn't used their burn barrel in several days. That's all I know."

"And it suddenly began burning again? That's rather frightening."

"Yes." There was another long pause and Ashley yawned again. "Seems as if it's been ages since we talked—about other stuff, I mean. I've got chocolate chip cookies!"

"C'mon over then," I said. "My still-gray hair'll be dry in a couple of minutes. Coffee's on. Sounds as if you need some caffeine."

"Okay!" Ashley giggled and clicked off and I climbed over Rowdy, who was sprawled in the hallway, so I could get to the bathroom and my hair dryer.

A few minutes later, Ashley was knocking on the front door, and I opened it to let her in, accompanied by a gust of cold wind and a flurry of snow.

"Whew!" she exclaimed, holding out a plate covered in aluminum foil. She shed coat, hat and mittens, and stomped to get the snow off her boots. "It's a cold one today!"

"You can throw your boots over there." I pointed at a rug by the coat stand. "Want a pair of slippers?"

"No, I've got on heavy socks." Ashley sat down and pulled off her boots, tossing them onto my boot rug. "Can't wait to have some cookies!" she said, then, "Hey, Rowdy!"

Rowdy opened one eye, gave her a polite look, and went back to sleep.

"Laziest dog on the planet," Ashley remarked, bending to scratch my dog behind his ear.

"He has his moments," I said. "I'll get coffee." I set the cookies on the coffee table and gave Rowdy a stern look, but he appeared to be safely oblivious to the delights of Ashley's cookies.

Ashley trailed behind me into the kitchen and watched while I fetched cups—my favorites, in the Blue Willow pattern my grandmother loved—and poured coffee for each of us.

"So, what's up?" I asked, setting the coffeepot back in the coffeemaker.

"You've got a new neighbor," Ashley answered, moving back into the living room and plumping down on a chair. She tossed her long blonde braid over her shoulder and reached for a cookie. "The Abbott house is sold."

"Really?" I carried the coffee into the living room. The Abbott house had figured prominently in the excitement over the robbery last fall. "I thought Mrs. Abbott was keeping her home."

"Nope. Matt knows Marcy Abbott, Mrs. Abbott's niece, and she said one of Mrs. Abbott's kids told her that the house was too hard to keep an eye on from where they live in Ohio. They said Olivia was pretty upset about the robbery, and she's having fun with the grandkids. So they sold it through a friend's realty. That's why there was no For Sale sign."

I blinked, trying to follow Ashley's tale of who told whom what. Bottom line, I decided, was that Olivia Abbott was living in Ohio with her kids, and she had decided to sell her house. Ashley's husband, Matt, had heard the news and told his wife.

"It's a beautiful place with all those gables. I suppose it wasn't too hard to find a buyer." I sat down across from Ashley, snagged a cookie and slid a mug in her direction.

Ashley picked it up and took a sip. "So the new people are city-citizens from Chicago. A woman and her mom. The mom has some health issues, but she grew up just down the road from here in Prairie City, so her daughter thought it would be good to bring her back here. You know, to an area where she was familiar with things. Matt said Marcy Abbott said that Olivia knew the buyers from when she used to live in Ohio. She's got a cat."

I sighed. Following Ashley's train of thought could be somewhat challenging, especially with the interesting turns of phrase she often threw into her narratives—'city-citizens' being a favorite. "Who has a cat?" I asked. "Marcy or ..."

Ashley giggled. "The people moving into the Abbott house. I wonder what they'll think of Rowdy."

"Rowdy wouldn't chase a cat," I said quickly.

"Of course not. But he *is* a big boy." She glanced down the hallway to where Rowdy was still deep in doggy slumber, looking for all the world like a black bear rug. "Their names are Rose and Leila Hartin. Matt said Marcy said Rose—that's the mom—has early Alzheimer's, and Leila has to keep a careful eye on her. " She put her chin in her hand. "I wonder if either of them knows how to embroider?"

I laughed. "They might, at that. I'll go pay them a visit and introduce myself once they're moved in. It'll be good to get to know some more people in Burtonville."

"Oh, you'll get a chance to meet a bunch of people during the quilt project!" crowed Ashley. "They're expecting a pretty big turnout on Sunday, and there's a potluck. Did I say that?"

"Don't think so," I said.

"Well, there is. Bring that lava cake you make. And add extra chocolate. Maybe make it mocha."

"Okay," I said meekly, and Ashley grinned. "Strawberries?" I asked.

"Raspberries. Oh yes, and chocolate shavings."

"You got it."

Ashley grinned. "I'll give you a raincheck on the wallpapering since you're baking."

"Good deal," I said. "Lava cake priority."

Ashley and I finished our coffee in perfect harmony, both of us thinking of Sunday and potlucks, and, most particularly, of lava cake.

Chapter Three

The Saturday movie line-up was execrable. Nothing to see but comedy, which I hated; action-adventure, which Duffy hated; and heavy drama, which Louise loathed—so we gave up on the idea of the cinema and went instead to *Fibber McGee*'s, our favorite sea food restaurant.

"Can you guys embroider?" I asked, my mouth full of shrimp cocktail.

"Embroider?" asked Louise.

"Embroider?" echoed Duffy. "Where'd that question come from?"

I tossed a shrimp tail into the bowl in the center of the table and reached for some more cocktail sauce. "Burtonville has a winter community project going. They're putting together a quilt with blocks for historical landmarks. I think we should all do one."

"I can help," said Louise. "Hopefully, the patterns aren't too hard."

Duffy was looking at me wide-eyed. "I've never embroidered before. I'm not even sure I know what sort of needle to use. And where would we get the supplies, and how do you even do it? I don't think I'm a good candidate."

"You can knit," I pointed out.

"Well, yes," he said. "But ..."

I grinned at the look of consternation on his face. In fact, Duffy had created some beautiful knitted scarves, my favorite being a lavender cable-knit that my stepdaughter Natalie wore every winter.

"What's the timeline?" asked Louise. "I've got a heavy teaching load this semester, you know."

"Dunno," I answered. "There's an organizing party on Sunday. Want to come?"

"Oh dear, I've got a ton of grading to do ..."

"Lava cake," I said.

"I'm in," she said promptly.

"I can't join you," said Duffy. "I told my neighbors I'd help them pack. They're moving to an apartment. It'd be rude to back out now."

"That's all right. We'll get all the details and I'll send you a square to work on."

"I'm not sure ..."

"It'll be fine, Duffy. Don't fret about it," I said, but I could tell he was fretting. He had scrunched up his forehead and run his fingers through his hair, a sure sign of agitation. Louise looked at me and raised her brows, so I said, "Really, if you don't want to, you don't have to. It doesn't matter that much."

"I just want it to be right," he said, frowning.

"Knowing you, it'll be right," I said soothingly. "But, really, no obligation."

"I'll do it," he said. "But no promises on what it'll look like."

"Relax, Duffy," I exclaimed. "It doesn't have to be a work of art. Just a quilt block. I'll get the patterns and you can decide. Check the Internet. There's tons of stuff on embroidery." *I hope,* I thought.

Louise put her hand up to her mouth to hide a grin.

"Dessert, anyone?" I asked, to change the subject.

"Of course!" said Louise, but Duffy sat back in his chair and patted his belly.

"I better not. I ate too many crab legs. I'm done with eating for a while." He signaled the server. "We've got two dessert takers here," he said when she looked over. "Hey, did you ever figure out what animal that was the other night?"

Louise looked at me, her eyebrows raised. "Animal?"

"Actually, no, I didn't. And I haven't heard it since," I answered.

"Animal?" Louise said again, a little more loudly.

"Marianne and I heard the oddest sound when we were out stargazing," Duffy said. "Almost like something howling."

"Howling?" Louise said. "In Burtonville? Was it a dog?"

"No, not like a dog howling," I said, frowning. "Maybe more like moaning, or … or something. It was a ways away."

Louise leaned across the table, her pretty brow furrowed in mock worry. "Any clanking chains?" she asked in a stage whisper.

Duffy smiled. "No chains. Just moans, a moan—or whatever. It was a creepy sound. Marianne and I even went out and looked around for a while. I've been wondering what it could've been."

"Ooh!" Louise squeaked. "A mystery!"

In truth, I'd been wondering about it as well. I was reminded when I let Rowdy out the night before, and I shut the door a little more quickly than I might otherwise have done. "Hmm," I said. "I'll ask Ashley. She might know. I saw her the other day, but we were talking about—um—other things."

Louise laughed. "I bet you were. Anything you *didn't* talk about?"

"Not that I remember," I remarked, and Louise laughed again. "But here's a bit of news," I went on. "That fire the other night?" Duffy nodded. "It might have been set deliberately."

"Really?" Duffy asked. "What burned?"

"It was a pile of trash, but it's being treated as suspicious," I answered.

"In Burtonville? That seems a bit far-fetched."

I shrugged. "I heard it straight from the source."

"Ashley?" asked Louise.

"Yep."

Louise and I decided to be sensible and split an order of fried ice cream, which we devoured with gusto while Duffy looked on. When we finally got up to leave, I was a bit sorry about the dessert, because I'd eaten more seafood than was probably wise, and the fried ice cream wasn't sitting well.

"Wow, I'm stuffed," I said, as Louise and I watched Duffy walk to his car. "Want to go hike around the mall and work some of this off?"

"Sure," answered Louise. "Let's take my car."

Soon I was settled in her red Taurus, and my friend got out to scrape the windshield. It was another cold day, with wind whipping across the flat landscape. To distract myself from the dismal prospect of more months of this weather, I began to imagine my summer garden. Ashley, who had a splendid green thumb, had promised to help me, as gardening was definitely not my area of expertise. I was glad I could land a hand with her wallpapering and home renovations. I was just starting to visualize a whole corner of yellow mums in my summer secret garden when Louise climbed breathlessly back into the car.

"Stinking weather," she grumbled, tossing her scraper into a side pocket of the car door. "That wind is just brutal. Time to find a new inside project."

"Embroidery?" I offered, and smiled.

"Embroidery works," said Louise, then added, "Poor Duffy."

I sighed. "He doesn't have to help. I tried to tell him that."

Louise glanced at me as she maneuvered her car out of the parking lot. "He adores you, you know. If it's got to do with you, then he'll give it his best.'"

"He adores me usually. He was an ass last fall." Duffy had been unenthusiastic, to put it mildly, about my move to Burtonville, and it had turned into a pretty serious row.

"He was an ass last fall," agreed Louise. "You ever going to forgive him?"

"I have forgiven him," I said quickly. "Oh, Louise, it's complicated. You know that. Let's not start this conversation for the zillionth time."

"Has it only been a zillion? Imagine that." Louise clucked her tongue.

I crossed my arms, and we carefully guided the conversation to other topics. The walk in the mall was fun—and also therapeutic, since I felt as if I could actually fit behind the wheel of my Prius by the time we returned to *Fibber McGee*'s to get my car.

"See you Sunday," I called to Louise and hustled to get inside my vehicle before the wind blew my hat off. It was a little under half an hour back to Burtonville, so I turned my car heater and my radio on high, and was soon rolling along the road humming happily to an old *Cat Stevens* song. Then my attention was caught by two things.

First, a large van had turned off the freeway and was traveling down the two-lane road behind me toward Burtonville. I watched it idly in my rearview mirror, wondering if it was the new owners bringing their things to the Abbott place.

Next, a Sheriff's vehicle with its lights flashing appeared, followed closely by an ambulance. They sped up the road behind the van, waiting to get past. The sirens began to wail. I quickly turned on my emergency blinkers and pulled as far off the side of the road as I could, given the piles of snow, watching the van do the same. I didn't envy the driver negotiating a narrow, wintery road with an emergency vehicle hurrying to get by. But soon we were both safely out of the way and the two vehicles rocketed past. I spied Officer Brad Stanton at the wheel of the Sheriff's car, but he didn't glance my way and I didn't try to signal. Soon the taillights had faded into the distance, and I frowned, wondering what was happening in my little town.

I maneuvered the Prius back into my lane and watched the van do likewise, then I drove off down the road as fast as the blowing snow would allow. Fifteen minutes later, I was approaching Burtonville, and I felt my pulse leap in alarm. There were flashing lights on Beale Street, and that meant one of my close neighbors was in trouble. *Please not the Middens,* I said under my breath.

But the ambulance was parked alongside the curb in front of the Abbott home—not by Ashley's place, thank the Goddess. I pulled my Prius into the garage and climbed out, squinting at the flashing lights. I could see Officer Stanton standing by his vehicle, his collar turned up against the wind.

Several of the residents with homes along Beale Street were outside and watching, coats and hats clutched around them.

Ashley ran up to me.

"What happened?" I exclaimed.

"It's one of the Hartins," answered Ashley. "I've been listening to the police radios, but I can't really tell what's going on. Matt just went over there."

Just then Ashley's phone buzzed and she grabbed it out of her pocket.

"That's Matt," she said. "I'll call you later, okay? And if not, tomorrow at the church?"

"Tomorrow," I said. "And let me know if there's anything I can do to help," I called after her as she hurried away down the sidewalk.

Ashley looked over her shoulder and waved, and I made my way inside to the relative warmth and peace of my home. I had meant to ask her about the noise Duffy and I heard, but decided that under the circumstances, it could wait.

Chapter Four

With my 'Lava Cake for a Crowd' recipe safely returned to my recipe file and the delicious aroma of chocolate wafting through my little house, I sat down in my study the next morning and began looking for online tutorials that would reacquaint me with embroidery before the community gathering.

The worst video I found was a computer-generated monotone over an animated slideshow, replete with occasional tinkling music—again computer-generated—that made my eardrums cringe. The best was 'Eleanor's Embroidery Excellence,' a series of lessons by a young woman who appeared close to the age of my stepdaughter, Natalie, and for a while, I was quite literally lost in Eleanor's beautiful work. She was so accomplished in the art that her stitchery could have been mistaken for an oil painting; yet, she patiently walked through hoops and needles, stem stitch and running stitch, tying off and blocking, looking so earnest and adept that even I was convinced there was hope for my needlecraft.

By the time I logged off and began gathering up to head to the church, I was confident I could hold up my end of an embroidery conversation, and that would be adequate for now. I could practice, after all, on fabric scraps. I popped the warm lava cake into a cake carrier, wrapped the carrier in four or five layers of towels in the hope that they might help ward off the cold, and then set the whole thing into my picnic basket, just as my phone rang and Ashley announced she was on the way to pick me up.

Rowdy watched me dolefully from the kitchen door, but when I explained to him that chocolate wasn't good for dogs, but that I'd bring him home a special something for his dinner, he cheered up and went back to the living room to lie in his favorite spot by the door.

The Methodist church was a lovely red brick structure on the edge of town, artistically draped in icicles and with the front walk carefully shoveled and salted. A stream of people was headed inside, lugging slow cookers and casserole dishes and sewing totes, and two small children tussled under the drooping branches of a tall spruce tree growing near the church cemetery. I spied the Paulsens and the Burtons, both from Beale Street, along with several other faces I recognized.

"Wow, there are a lot of people here," I commented to Ashley.

"Lots of quilt squares to go around," she answered. "And everyone loves a potluck, even if they aren't sewing."

"Yes, I suppose," I said, but my enthusiasm for the project—despite Eleanor's encouraging videos—was waning. The pressure would be on to create something presentable, and I wasn't sure my crafting skills were up to par.

"Hi guys!" Louise panted up, carrying a big bowl filled with Asian salad. "Quite a turnout!"

I nodded glumly, but Louise wasn't deterred, and she and Ashley began chatting happily while we shed our outdoor gear and I looked around for the dessert table. I was slightly cheered by the fact that the lava cake still felt acceptably warm, despite the car trip and another bitingly cold day. We'd had the heater blasting in the car for the short drive to the church, but I didn't think the temperature outside had managed to edge above ten degrees.

Soon everyone had a plate piled high with food, and the church pastor offered a short grace. Next, a middle-aged man sporting a checked coat stepped to the front of the room and fastened a cordless microphone to the front of his jacket. Ashley and Louise sat down next to me and Ashley nudged me.

"That's the mayor," she whispered. "Bill Yadley."

"Hello everyone!" the mayor boomed. "We're delighted at the great crowd today. I'll just take a second to explain the project, and then we can get down to eating. In a few minutes, Mandy is going to come to the tables to distribute patterns and fabric blocks. The patterns all represent historical aspects of Burtonville, and we hope you'll pick one that means something special to you. If you're newer to Burtonville ..." Mayor Yadley's eyes flicked around the room, "... then Mandy or I would be happy to help with some background. Or for that matter, so would your friends and neighbors," he added, as a chorus of voices chimed in. "We'd like to begin piecing together the project on April 1st, so we ask that you all complete your quilt squares no later than March 15th. You can turn them in here at the church, or give them to Mandy or me at the town hall any Tuesday afternoon between 3 and 6 PM."

"Mandy?" I queried Ashley in an undertone.

"Township clerk," she whispered. "Mandy Patterson."

"You're welcome to use your own materials," Mayor Yadley went on. "But if you need supplies and don't have them, please let me or Mandy know. We have needles and yarn—"

"Floss," corrected Mandy.

"Floss." The mayor grinned. "And those looms—" He glanced at Mandy.

"Hoops," said Mandy promptly.

"Hoops! Yes, hoops. We have needles, floss, and hoops at the township hall. Please don't sign your square, but when you turn it in—before March 15th, don't forget!—just pin a paper with your name and telephone number on your work. We'll make a map of the squares so we're sure we have everyone's contribution recognized."

Mandy picked up several folders and started toward the first table.

"Thank you, everyone! Now dive in!" the mayor boomed.

There was a collective clatter of forks as people began to shovel down piles of delicious food.

"Did I tell you the new family is moving into the Abbott's?" I said to Louise. "I saw the moving truck coming into town. I guess they have a cat. I wonder what kind?"

"What was that?" A shrill voice came from down the table and I craned my head to look. A sharp-faced woman with unlikely red hair was glaring down at me, her eyebrows drawn down. She clutched a fork as if it was a weapon, and held it speared on a piece of broccoli.

"I beg your pardon?" I said.

"What did you say?" she repeated and pointed at me with a red-tipped fingernail. I saw the man seated next to her edge a few inches away from her. He handed a muffin to a little girl with lava cake smeared on her cheeks.

"No more cake," he said, "until you've had some regular food."

I looked at Ashley. I had spoken quietly and was astonished anyone had heard me in the hubbub of collective eating. She shrugged and mouthed, *Tell you later*.

"Are you talking to me?" I tried to make my tone polite.

"Yes!" the woman exclaimed and began to rise from her chair. "What did you say about the Abbott house?"

"Um," I said. "I mentioned that the new owners are moving in and that I saw a truck."

"But the cat. You said they had a cat."

"I heard that they did, yes." I couldn't resist another glance at Ashley, who had started the cat rumor. "I saw a particolored tortie on the corner of Beale and Myrtle," barked the woman. "Out in the cold. Shocking lack of care. It ran under the porch at the old Abbott place."

"Oh, I don't know ..." I began, but she cut me off.

"Appalling that they'd let a cat out in these conditions when they haven't even moved in yet," she spluttered. "Unpardonable."

I sat back and exchanged glances with Louise, whose thunderstruck expression would have been funny if the situation hadn't been so awkward. It was very cold for a cat to be left out of doors, but I had no evidence that Leila and Rose Hartin's cat had even arrived in Burtonville at all, let alone being the one that had been spied running under the porch. What was more, I hadn't yet talked with Ashley about why there had been an ambulance at the house. Were the Hartins moving in yet or not? I turned doggedly to my cheesy potatoes, hoping to discourage further conversation.

Out of the corner of my eye, I saw the red-haired woman lean forward as if she wanted to continue her diatribe, but, to my relief, Mandy

Patterson arrived at our table and distracted everyone's attention. She handed the folder of quilt block patterns to Ashley.

Ashley and Louise opened the folder and I looked over their shoulders, pretending to be engrossed with sorting through them. After staring down at me for several moments, the woman went back to her food, stabbing with her fork at a pile of green beans. Relieved, I turned my attention to the quilt blocks.

"I'm taking this one," announced Louise, holding up a drawing of the Burtonville water tower.

Ashley picked up two pages. "I'm torn," she said. "I like this one of the garden club window boxes, but it seems sort of hard."

I looked over her shoulder. "What about that one?" I pointed to a drawing of a big house with a hexagonal structure in the back. Ashley flipped past it. "Wait, what was that?" I asked, snagging the piece of paper and pulling it out of the pile. "That's the old house south of town, isn't it? I recognize it, but not the other building."

Ashley threw an anxious sidelong glance across the table, and I looked up. A small gray-haired woman was smiling at us.

"Oh, I can tell you what that is," she said, smiling. "I used to live there."

"You used to live in that big house?" Louise asked politely. "It's a lovely place, and such an unusual ... well, what is that behind the house?"

"It's a barn," the woman answered. "Bethany Probst." She leaned across the table and held out her hand for a quick handshake. "I'm Bethany Probst. I used to be Bethany Forrest, but not anymore."

Ashley cleared her throat.

I glanced at Ashley. "Nice to meet you," I said. "I'm Marianne Reed, and these are—"

"Oh, I know Ashley Midden. Her husband's on the fire team. "He helped when ... oh, you know."

"Yes," said Ashley softly.

"This is Louise Klein," I pushed on, feeling undertones, but not sure where they were coming from. "So, you lived in this pretty house?"

The red-haired woman had looked up from her green beans and was glaring down the table at us again. I tried to ignore her.

"Yes, I did," said Bethany Probst. "I and ... oh, five or six, or sometimes more children. We had twelve at one time. My angels, my little stars."

I felt a slow sinking in the area of my belly. The house was a ruin now and the barn was long gone. "You had twelve children?" I asked, trying to change the subject.

"Oh yes!" she said and smiled again. I saw the red-haired cat lady throw a stony look in her direction. "We had lots of children, Mr. Forrest and I. Well, not ours, but lost souls, lost little children needing somewhere to be. We took care of all of them, and oh, I miss them—my sweet ones."

I swallowed, hoping Mrs. Probst wouldn't start to weep. Her faded brown eyes were the most melancholy I had ever seen.

"Did you find one you liked?" Mandy wandered back over from where she'd been talking to the little girl with the lava cake face paint, and I turned with difficulty away from the sad-faced Bethany Probst.

"I'm going to stick with the window box," said Ashley.

"Um." I looked at Bethany and asked, "Did you want to do this one of ... um ... the house where you lived?"

"Oh, no. You take that one, dear," Mrs. Probst answered, and reached for her fork.

Feeling awkward, I picked up two pages at random and added the one with the house and the unusual barn. "I'll take these three. One for me, one for my stepdaughter, and one for my friend," I told Mandy. I glanced down at the pictures, hoping I hadn't chosen anything too difficult. Natalie, who didn't even know she'd been drafted yet, and Duffy would kill me.

"And how about you, Bethany?" Mandy asked. Bethany held up her page. It was a storefront, an old Ten Cent store that I presumed had once graced Main Street.

"Wonderful!" Mandy said. "At this rate, we're going to get all the squares handled!" She strode away with her folder and went to the next table.

Bethany Probst stood up. "Very nice to meet you both," she said, nodding at me and Louise. "I'm going to start for home now. So cold outside for walking! Goodbye, Ashley!"

"Bye, Bethany," Ashley said and helped arrange her chair back under the table.

"She's walking?" I whispered to Ashley, and Ashley nodded.

"She's out walking a lot," she answered, and when I opened my mouth to protest, added, "Yes, even in this cold."

We watched as she made her way to the salad table and picked up a small bowl, then disappeared out the door in the direction of the coat room.

"I've never seen a sadder looking woman!" I said softly to Ashley.

The red-haired woman had turned her sharp gaze in my direction as soon as Bethany Probst took her leave, and I feared she was going to begin the cat conversation again. The table dynamics were definitely not to my liking. I wished she'd gone home rather than Bethany Probst.

"You don't know the half of it," replied Ashley. "It's a long, depressing story. Let me help clean up and then we can have a chat. When there are fewer people," she added, and didn't look in the direction of the red-haired woman, but I knew whom she meant.

Chapter Five

"I'm going to say goodbye as well," said Louise, gathering up her dishes and the empty bowl that had held her Asian salad. "I have work to do, and I don't want to be on the roads after dark if I can help it. I'll call you later, Marianne."

She gave me a hug and flapped her hand at Ashley, who was helping the church staff collect salt and pepper shakers and fold tablecloths. Ashley grinned. "See you soon," she said. "Have fun with your quilt block!"

"Can't wait to get started," replied Louise. "And Marianne, fill me in on what Duffy says. If he's uncomfortable with doing his square, I can help."

"Okay," I said. Ashley walked past and I fell into step with her. "Can't believe I forgot to ask you. Did you find out what happened at the Abbott place?"

Ashley rolled up a tablecloth for washing while I rescued a spoon and several paper napkins that had fallen on the floor, putting them on the tray

I was carrying. "It was Rose Hartin," Ashley commented. "She had a bad spell."

"Is she okay?"

"I guess she's fine. She and Leila came to meet the moving truck, but Rose got dizzy and was talking funny. Leila was scared she might've had a stroke. Apparently Rose was kind of agitated. Maybe because of seeing the new house or something."

"That's so sad," I commented. "I hope living there won't be too much for Rose."

"Me too," said Ashley. "It's a friend moving them in, so they'll just leave the van parked 'til Rose is better and they can finish the job. Leila took Rose home and they're going to give it a few days to make sure she's okay."

"What happened to the cat?" came a sharp voice from behind Ashley. She jumped, and I saw irritation flash across her face–an unusual reaction for Ashley, who was perpetually good-natured.

My eyes flew to the red-haired woman. She had come up unnoticed and was listening in on our conversation.

"What?" Ashley turned toward her.

"I said, what happened to the cat? Did they take the cat with them?"

"What cat?"

"Their cat—the tortie I saw. They left it out in the cold."

Ashley took a breath, I thought fighting for patience. "I don't know about any cat. I'd be surprised if it's theirs. They aren't even moved in.

Are you sure it doesn't have a home in one of the other houses on Beale Street?"

The woman sighed. Without another word, she turned her back on us and started for the coat rack. A man holding a little boy by the hand was blocking the passageway, and she pushed past them rudely, knocking the man's arm. She jerked her jacket off the hanger, glared over her shoulder at us, and slammed out the door. Ashley and I stared after her.

"What in the world?" I said.

Ashley frowned. "That woman is certifiable. She gets obsessed with things. Right now, it's cats. And she has a terrible temper. Gets in quarrels with everyone about nothing."

"What's her name?"

"Nancy Brock. She lives just across the street. The humane society visited her a bit ago and removed some of the cats in her house. She's got more than she can take care of, and if she sees a cat on the street, she picks it up. Doesn't matter if it has an owner. If you get a cat, keep it away from her. Otherwise, it'll disappear."

"I'm pretty much a confirmed dog owner," I assured Ashley. "But I hope she doesn't pester the Hartins. It sounds as if they have plenty to contend with."

I followed Ashley into the kitchen and dumped the tray of silverware into the sink. The mayor had his sleeves rolled up and was carefully loading the dishwasher.

"Anything else we can do to help clean up?" Ashley asked.

"No, you two go home before it gets any colder," said Mayor Yadley.

So Ashley and I wandered back to our table and I picked up my picnic basket and the lava cake tin. I regarded the quilt block patterns. "I need to look these over and think about who should embroider which," I commented. "I hope I didn't pick ones that are too hard!"

Ashley touched the picture of the house with the hexagonal barn. "I was going to tell you the story of that one."

"Yes," I said. "I felt badly about taking it. I thought maybe Mrs. Probst might want it."

"Oh, I doubt it," said Ashley. "Let's go sit down for a minute. We can talk a bit before we brave the weather again."

I followed her to an empty table and sat down next to her. Ashley put her chin in her hand. "So, Bethany Probst—she was Bethany Forrest then—lived in that big house for about fifteen years. When they came to Burtonville, she and her husband had three kids ... or maybe four ... I can't remember for sure. They were all foster kids, and Bethany doted on them. They were good kids—got good grades in school, always well-dressed and well-behaved. And then they took in some more children, and some more, and I think at one point they had eight or so. But then things started to get not-so-good."

"Uh oh," I said. "Eight kids is a lot. I thought she said twelve, though."

"I don't think there were ever twelve. At least not all at one time. She gets confused sometimes."

"Eight is still a bunch of kids."

"Yes, but there was plenty of room in their house, and they seemed to collect them. Kids without a place to go just wandered in. That place is huge. But one of the boys they took in was really wild. He beat up a couple of his classmates and vandalized the old post office. Then one night he got some beer from somewhere-or-other, stole a car, wrecked it, got arrested. And while all that was going on, apparently Bill Forrest, Bethany's husband, was getting fed up. He started running around ... you can guess the rest."

"He left her?"

"Eventually. But not after there were some spectacular scenes. Their son got arrested again, and ended up in juvie for a while. After he got out, things seemed to settle down for a little bit and then that old barn burned right to the ground one night. A lot of people thought Noah had done it—that was the one boy that was causing so much trouble. But, actually, by then several of the other kids were troublemakers. Bill and Bethany divorced and then the kids all ended up moving out or into other homes, and it just about killed Bethany, I think. She looked like a zombie for months."

I looked down at my hands, which were clenched tightly in my lap. Tragedy came in all shapes and sizes, and it sounded as if Bethany Probst had her share. “Where does she live now?”

“In a room—a little apartment—just a block or so from you.” I hid a smile. Everyone in Burtonville lived a block or so away from everyone else. “We were pretty surprised,” Ashley went on, “that she didn’t leave Burtonville after all her trouble, but she didn’t. She told Matt she raised her children here, and so here she’ll stay. Keeps to herself. Doesn’t go out all that much except for walking. It’s actually pretty surprising that she was here today.”

I shook my head. There was a lump in the back of my throat. “I feel really terrible,” I said. “I hope I didn’t distress her with my stupid questions about that drawing.”

“It’s been a few years,” Ashley said reassuringly. “She didn’t seem upset.”

“I hope not. Maybe I’ll pay her a visit,” I said. “It sounds as if she’s had a really terrible time.” I imagined her sitting in her room, thinking of the past and of her children, all alone with her sadness, and it made me want to cry.

Interpreting rightly that my mood had taken a turn for the worse, Ashley quipped, “So, you got to meet a few Burtonvillains. Hope you weren’t disappointed!”

“I feel as if I spent most of my time eating,” I said, trying to shake off the melancholy vision. “I didn’t get to talk to that many people.”

“We’ll have some more get-togethers, don’t worry,” said Ashley.

"That'd be nice. In the meantime, I found some videos online and I need to go check them out again. I'm beginning to wonder if I got myself in over my head."

Ashley laughed. "Nope. It'll be fun. Invite Natalie to visit, and we can embroider the night away."

"Good idea," I said.

I shrugged into my coat, set the quilt square patterns carefully in my picnic basket atop the empty lava cake pan, and bent to pull on my boots.

Outside, I could hear people calling and laughing and cars starting up. It was time to go home and feed Rowdy, and 'fess up to Natalie and Duffy about what I'd gotten them into.

Chapter Six

I was awakened that night by a *Woof!* from Rowdy, alarming enough in itself, but also by the howling of sirens again. Fumbling for my glasses, I turned on the bedside lamp, swung out of bed, stuffed my feet into slippers and hurried through the darkened living room to peer out my front window.

Across the street was bedlam, people rushing back and forth, lights flashing. There were at least three emergency vehicles that I could see, and a small structure was consumed in fire. I recognized it as the shed behind the Abbott—now Hartin—house, flames clawing skyward nearly as tall as the second-floor window of the house, and a heavy pall of smoke hanging over the big yard. The van still sat in the drive, well away from the fire, fortunately.

The residents of Burtonville had poured out into the street and were huddled in little clusters by the curb, garbed in heavy coats over bathrobes, their feet jammed into boots, their breaths raising clouds of steam.

I peered at my watch. Just past midnight. Clipping on Rowdy's leash, I decided to join the crowd and see what had happened. Soon we were standing outside in the bitter cold, amidst streams of water shooting into the burning building, calls and shouts from the fire team, and flashing blue and red lights. It was so cold that the air seared my lungs, and the heat from the roaring fire almost felt good on my face. Ashley hurried over and stood next to me.

"How did it start?" I asked her.

"No one knows. But the shed is a complete loss. Matt's likely to be here a while before it's all put out. I'm glad of the snow because there's a bunch of deadfall and dry grass back there. The house could easily have caught fire as well. Even so, Hartins are going to have quite a mess to clean up."

"I feel sorry for them." I sighed. "This hasn't exactly been a very pleasant move-in. First Rose ... that's the mom, right?"

"Right," said Ashley.

"First Rose has a bad spell," I went on, "and now this. I hope they don't give up on Burtonville."

"I hope not, too," said Ashley, glancing at the van still parked in the drive. "They haven't even had the chance to unload." Then, "There's Matt!" she cried, and trotted over to talk to her husband.

There was a crash and I jumped back as a shower of sparks shot up into the night sky to mingle with the stars as the shed roof caved in, but under the relentless jets of water soon the flames died down to a smolder and steam began to billow. I reached down and patted Rowdy, where he stood leaning against my leg. My feet and hands were beginning to ache, and I wondered if Rowdy's paws were cold.

"Let's go home, my man," I said. Giving his leash a tug, I turned to head for the house.

"Marianne!"

I stopped and looked over my shoulder. Striding toward us was Officer Brad Stanton of the Prairie City Sheriff's Department, the handsomest man on the planet, if not in the galaxy, though his dark hair was mussed and lines of worry creased his forehead. He had his hands stuffed deep in the pockets of his blue jacket, and the tip of his aristocratically-chiseled nose was pink, none of which diminished his beauty in any way. He would be drop dead gorgeous if he'd been rolling in a pig wallow.

"Hi, Brad," I greeted him. "Bad night for a fire. *Strange* night for a fire, with all this snow. Want to come in for a cup of something warm? Rowdy and I were about to call it a night—or perhaps a morning."

Brad glanced around and gave a small smile. "Guess I've got enough help to control the crowds. Sure, a cup of something would be very welcome. Technically, I'm not on duty, but I came when the fire alarm sounded."

He gave Rowdy a scratch, and then followed me across the street to my little house, rubbing his hands together and then stuffing them back in his pockets.

It was blessedly warm inside. Rowdy padded off to get a drink of water and thump down on his favorite rug. I handed him a chew bone, and then left Brad to shed his coat and boots, bustling into my bedroom to put on some presentable clothing. Like my neighbors, the other Burtonvillains, I had gone out with my winter coat over my pajamas.

"Coffee?" I called to Brad, pulling on jeans and a pair of sneakers. "Or hot chocolate, maybe?"

"Hot chocolate sounds wonderful," he answered. I pulled on jeans, dug out a sweatshirt, stuffed my feet into a pair of warm socks, and walked out of the bedroom to find him inspecting the telescope that was still parked in the corner of my living room. "This is a beauty. Is it yours?"

"Heavens, no. I could never afford that, let alone schlep it around. It belongs to a friend of Duffy's. He's an astronomer at the U, and he loaned it to us to do some stargazing."

"Wow," said Brad. "Great of him to let you borrow it. I love stargazing."

I hesitated. The polite thing to do was to invite him to join us sometime, but there was the possibility of some awkwardness. He and Duffy had hit it off like a couple of old pals, but Brad had told me he'd like to get to know me better and I knew his interest in me wasn't just as *friends*. Aside from a couple of quick dinners together, things hadn't gone any farther than that. Why, I wasn't sure. Was it some foot-dragging on my part? Whatever the cause, I didn't feel ready for the social maneuvering that could result from a night under the stars with the two of them.

I compromised by saying, "I'm not sure how long we'll be able to keep the equipment, but I'll let you know if there's another opportunity."

Brad smiled, and I went into the kitchen. I measured hot chocolate into my Blue Willow mugs and put the kettle on the stove, while Brad propped his tall frame against the kitchen door and regarded me with his coffee-colored eyes. He looked troubled.

"You look as if you have something on your mind," I commented.

"Yeah," he said. There was a short silence. Then, "Too many fires lately for my comfort. Not just here. In Peoria and in Prairie City, too."

I glanced at him but didn't comment.

Brad shifted his weight and frowned thoughtfully. "Marianne, you haven't noticed any kids hanging around here, have you? Not young kids, actually, but young adults—people you don't know? Twenty-somethings? Likely men, but there could also be young women."

"That's a little vague," I answered. "You'd be better off asking Ashley. There was a get-together at the church on Sunday and I was embarrassed by how many people I didn't know. In a town this size, I should be acquainted with more of my neighbors. I need to get out more or something."

"Well, you had some distractions when you moved in," Brad commented. "With the robbery and all."

"Agreed," I said. "But still."

"I think you would know if you saw the young people I'm talking about. They would stand out in a town like this. I'm sure Ashley knows all about this through Matt, anyway."

The kettle began to whistle, and I poured hot liquid into mugs, stirring to mix the chocolate. "Marshmallows?" I asked.

Brad wrinkled his nose. "No, thanks."

"Okay then. Not a marshmallow man." I laughed, thinking of Duffy, who liked marshmallows piled higher than the top of his mug. "Straight up for you." I set his mug on the kitchen table and gestured toward a chair, then sat down across from him.

He folded his hands around his cup. "Wow, that feels *so* good. I really hope this cold snap breaks soon. I'm not all that crazy about winter to start with, and this is really too much."

"Weather station says we'll have a break soon," I said. Then, "So what's this about kids?" I asked, moving the conversation back to the topic I was quite certain he'd come over to discuss in the first place.

He sighed. "It's just a hunch, but I've mentioned before that I'm a man who takes hunches seriously."

"Your gypsy ancestors," I said solemnly. "I remember."

"Right." He grinned.

Honestly, I thought, *no one should be allowed to be as attractive as he is*. That disarming smile, with his even, white teeth and the little laugh lines that formed by his eyes and his mouth, made my mind go every which way all on its own. I reeled it in sternly, and then reeled it in once or twice more, just to make sure I could pay attention to the conversation. A gorgeous man with a personality to match—not an easy combination to find.

I wondered if Brad had any idea what effect he had on people.

He looked up at the ceiling and sighed again, apparently oblivious to my straying thoughts. "We're following a street gang that is growing in strength over in Peoria and is into all sorts of mayhem. The Pyros is what they call themselves."

I grimaced. "The Pyros? I don't like where this is heading."

He frowned. "Yeah. Their routine involves ... Can you guess?"

"Well, it seems sort of obvious."

"Right?" he answered drily. "Fires. The Peoria police have been cracking down, but there's something about them—they've got a very charismatic leader—that is drawing a lot of young people in. They have clashed with a couple of the Peoria gangs—Zone 7 for one—and it's turning into a real problem. Unfortunately, one of the young men has connections to Burtonville, and I've just got a bad feeling."

"Who's that?" I asked. "What young man, I mean?"

"He was raised by a couple that used to live here—" Brad began, but stopped at the expression on my face.

"Don't tell me," I said. "Is his name Noah?"

"Noah, right. How'd you know?"

"Oh God," I said. I stood up and walked around my kitchen, clenching and unclenching my hands, the tragic vision of Bethany Probst swimming in front of my eyes. "I met his mother. That is, his foster mother, at that church event yesterday ..." I glanced at my watch. 2 AM. "Right ... yesterday. She lives here in Burtonville."

"Yes, she does," answered Brad, gazing at me. "Sad tale."

"Horrible," I said. "But I thought Noah had left?"

"He was in juvie. Twice, in fact, but he's been out for a while and now he's on our radar. One of the Prairie City officers stopped him driving this way a couple of days ago, nearly to Burtonville. Gave him a warning for a headlight out, but couldn't hold him for anything."

"Is it possible he was visiting his foster mom?" I asked. My stomach was churning. Bethany Probst—that poor woman. I set my mug in the sink and my hand shook a little.

"Possible, but not probable," answered Brad. "He doesn't seem to care about much of anyone or anything. He dropped out of sight for a bit, but now that he's resurfaced ... Well, there have been two suspicious fires right here in town."

"Two?"

“We’re pretty sure someone set this fire tonight,” Brad said.

“But why here?” I asked. “Why Burtonville?”

“Something to do with their ritual. Like breaking—or, rather, burning—ties with their old life. We’re pretty sure Noah’s behind at least some of the recent problems—here and in Peoria as well. Some of the fires in Peoria have been quite severe. Let’s hope it doesn’t spread to this small town. That shed fire could have been pretty serious.”

I gazed at Brad Stanton, feeling sick. *Please, please. Let Bethany not know*, I thought.

That same prayer went round and round in my head for the remainder of Brad’s visit, and it was still circling when I finally tumbled back into bed.

Chapter Seven

The world seemed slightly brighter the next morning, however, when my phone rang and I heard my stepdaughter's cheery voice on the other end of the line.

"What's this cell phone pic you sent?" Natalie asked.

"It's a quilt square," I answered, propping my phone under my ear so I could stir my oatmeal. "Burtonville's making an historic quilt."

"So, what're we doing?" Natalie giggled, and I laughed along with her.

"We've been drafted into making quilt blocks—you and I and Louise and Ashley and Duffy. They need 100 embroidered, and I figured...well, I figured you'd be a perfect candidate to do one."

"Who drafted me, Mummy?"

That was Natalie—straight to the point. "Um, Rowdy?" I tried, leaning over to look at him sprawled under the table. I kicked off my slipper and scratched his belly with my big toe. He opened one eye, gave a dreamy moan and went back to sleep.

Natalie snorted.

"Oh, okay. I did, and I also drafted Louise and Duffy, but I thought it would be sort of fun. And to be fair, Ashley drafted me. I was just spreading the joy. I thought we could have an embroidering bee. Maybe help each other out. I tried to pick a sort of simple pattern for you, but really, if you don't have time you should say 'no' and it'll be fine." I had a moment of consternation when I thought of doing two blocks on my own, especially if I had to rely on some of the instructional videos I'd found, but fortunately for me, Natalie is the world's best example of a good sport.

"When did you want to do it? The bee?" I could hear her tapping on her computer keyboard on the other end of the line. "I've got an abnormal psych paper due on Friday, and then things'll get crazy because my internship begins."

"The life of a graduate student is never dull," I commented.

"Nope," she said. "How 'bout this coming weekend? In between my paper and my internship starting. I could come Saturday and stay all night. Maybe do the bee Saturday evening?"

"I'll check with the gang," I said. "And if we can't get everyone here, you come anyway. Seems as if it's been ages."

"You didn't take my cat pictures down in my room, did you?"

"Never!" I exclaimed, smiling.

"That's a relief."

"Looking forward to seeing you, honey."

"Mwah," she said. "And give Rowdy one of those, too."

"I will." I looked down at my somnolent dog.

After Brad left, I'd had a disturbed rest of the night, full of dreams that I feared reflected some conflicted feelings about the men in my life. *Maybe I should stick with Rowdy,* I thought. *Less complicated.*

Natalie clicked off and I texted Louise, Duffy and Ashley to ask about a possible Saturday embroidery party, then yawned. It had not only been an interrupted night, it had been a short one. Making it an easy day would be sensible. I took my oatmeal off the stove, added some maple syrup and a little cream, and sat down to eat my brunch.

Rowdy lifted his head off the floor and gave me a tragic look. "None for you, my man," I told him. "You already had breakfast. But this evening, I'll take you to Leonard's for a burger, so don't despair."

The cold snap had finally broken, and the thermometer outside the kitchen window read 27 degrees—practically balmy. It would do both of us good to get out for a walk, and what better place to take him than Leonard's where they had the best pizza I had practically ever tasted, the ever-popular hamburgers that Rowdy devoured in one gulp of his big jaws, plus all sorts of other delicacies unusual for a small-town convenience store.

But first I was going to visit Bethany Probst, pay my respects, and see if I could urge her to come over for some dessert and a chat with Ashley and me, and my walk with Rowdy had to wait until a little later. I realized I had probably let the image of Bethany sitting alone and pining in a tiny, cramped room go to my head. The reality was likely far less dismal. Nonetheless, I had said I wanted to get to know some more of Burtonville's residents. Bethany Probst was first on the list.

When my oatmeal bowl was empty, and my third cup of coffee had chased the yawns away, I pushed back from the table, set my dishes in the sink and went to shower and change into jeans and a heavy sweater. I ran my fingers through my short curls, inspected what appeared to be some new silver strands growing at my temples, frowned and turned off the bathroom light.

I let Rowdy out to do his business, and, with a solemn promise that I hadn't forgotten his walk. donned my coat, hat and gloves. I went to Leonard's and bought a half dozen fresh croissants, and started down Main Street toward the house where Bethany Probst's apartment lay. With the weather a little warmer, the residents of Burtonville were out in numbers this morning, and I nodded and smiled at several people I had seen at the church gathering, again vowing to get out more. Burtonville had a lot of community events; I'd been so distracted with moving and my fall adventures that I hadn't been to any.

Soon I was turning toward Myrtle Street and walking up to a pretty gray clapboard house with red shutters and white curtains in the windows. A long porch crossed the front of the house, and a set of steep stairs led up the side of the home toward a door with an autumn wreath hanging askew against the screen. That didn't bode well for my fears about Bethany Probst—an elderly woman in a high apartment with outside stairs as an exit.

The stairs were shoveled, but could have used some salt. There were several icy spots that I had to navigate carefully. I glanced at my watch. 11:30 AM. A civilized time for a call, I hoped.

Seeing no doorbell, I knocked lightly and soon heard footsteps approaching. The door opened a crack and Mrs. Probst's face appeared in the opening, her hair rather tousled. She looked surprised when she saw me and immediately ran her hand down her clothing front, which I saw was a sprigged robe over the top of something checked—perhaps a pair of pajamas. So much for a civilized time to call.

"I hope I didn't wake you, Mrs. Probst," I stammered. "I should have called first."

"Oh, that's all right, dear."

I could tell she was searching for my name, so I supplied it. "Marianne Reed. I live on the next block, on Beale Street. We were together at the church meeting on Sunday?"

"Oh yes, of course!" she said and opened the door wider. "I'm sorry I'm not dressed. I don't sleep very well, and last night ... all those sirens! Mercy!"

Hesitating, I said, "I don't want to disturb you."

"Oh no! I don't get many visitors. I apologize for not being more presentable. Please come in!"

Her apartment wasn't a palace by any means, but certainly didn't match my nightmare vision of a cheerless cave. There were pictures on the walls, mainly of children, some toddlers, a few grown. One was of a younger Bethany with a gaggle of infants arrayed on a well-tended lawn.

She spied me looking at the photos and smiled, pointing at the babies. "That was a busy year, to be sure! Oh, all those weren't ours—just two of them—but there was a party for foster parents and a lot of infants in a lot of families. It was quite a time." She folded her arms and gazed at the photo, seeming lost in memories.

I cleared my throat. "I brought you some pastries," I said and held out the sack from Leonard's. "Sorry they aren't on a plate."

"Oh! Are they croissants?" Bethany said, peering into the bag. "I love them! I'll just go and put them out." She carried them into what I presumed was a small kitchen, and I took the opportunity to look around some more.

Worn furniture with antimacassars, a scratched coffee table, an open newspaper, a clock ticking away on the wall alongside the photos. It was a bit like a trip back in time, but everything was clean and neat and I realized, once again, that while Mrs. Probst probably had a lonely life, she was hardly living in barren squalor. It was simultaneously a relief and an embarrassment.

Mrs. Probst returned with a china tea pot and cups on a tray, carefully arranged with the pastries I had brought. I noticed that she had changed, tidied her hair and rubbed a bit of rouge on her cheeks. I had a quick recollection of my grandmother, who would never have ventured outside without her rouge.

But Bethany Probst wasn't really like my grandmother—she wasn't even the right age. In fact, she was probably younger than what my mother would have been, had she lived. She reminded me of both of them, somehow. I wondered if that was what had attracted me to her to start with. She seemed older than her actual years—acted older.

Mrs. Probst set the tray on the coffee table, folded the newspaper and sat down in the big chair, her feet crossed at the ankles. *Or perhaps she is like my grandmother,* I thought, remembering that prim lady hosting company in her living room.

"Please, sit down," she said, and I sank into a loveseat covered by a clean white sheet. "Ignore the covering," she said. "My cat likes to lie there, and—you know—all the hair."

"You have a cat?" I asked, thinking immediately of Nancy Brock.

"I do." Bethany Probst smiled. "She's an indoor-outdoor type. Out at the moment. I suppose she finds it a bit confining in this little apartment."

"What's she like?" I asked.

"Well, she's friendly, but won't come near anyone if she's outdoors. She wandered up here one day out of the blue. It was the strangest thing, her coming up all those stairs. I figured she was meant for me. I'm not really supposed to have a cat, but Bill—that's the man who lives downstairs and owns the house—is very deaf and never comes up. He has antique cars and is always fixing them and taking them to shows. He has a shop in his garage. I'm sure he has no idea she's here."

"What color is she?"

"Sort of orange and black mixed together. I can't remember what that's called."

"Tortoiseshell, I believe," I said. "I'm a dog person myself, but it sounds like that."

"Tortoiseshell—yes," Bethany nodded. "That's it."

I saw a particolored tortie on the corner of Beale and Myrtle, Nancy Brock had said. It had to be this cat. And if Nancy was creating trouble for Bethany Probst, I was not going to be happy.

I passed a pleasant hour with my neighbor, chatting about Burtonville, about my life in Peoria before I decided to move here, and about the quilt project. I debated inviting her to the bee on Saturday, decided against it, and then felt guilty.

On the one hand, it seemed as if she could use the company; on the other, I was looking forward to a cozy evening with the group of people I enjoyed most in the world, and I wasn't sure how well Mrs. Probst would fit in to a group that was already well-established and so close.

I gazed at her, sipping daintily at her tea and taking small bites of her croissant, and wondered what her life was like day-to-day. It wasn't an unpleasant environment in her apartment but seemed very solitary. Didn't any of her foster children visit her?

I had planned to avoid mentioning them, fearing it would make her unhappy, but she chattered away about them almost as if one or two might appear from the next room. It was a bit disconcerting. She gestured at a comforter folded neatly over the back of a straight chair in the corner.

"See the pattern on that?" she asked. "I crocheted it, and each one of the squares represents one of the children we raised. They all had their own colors, you know—or at least I imagined they did—so I gave each one a star in that color, and I can recite them all." She stood and walked over to it, pointing at the colorful squares. "Terry, Lawrence, Bron, Mandy, Alice, Amber, Mike, Latisha, Bobby ..." Her hand hovered over a teal block with a navy star. "And this one's Noah's. I miss him. I miss them all."

Noah. The young man who had caused so much trouble. The one suspected of fire-starting.

There was an uncomfortable silence, and then Bethany gave a little laugh. "You can see what I mean—one star for each. It helps me remember."

I shifted uncomfortably, wondering how to respond, but Mrs. Probst chatted on happily, turning the conversation to food and then to the weather, and I decided it was time to take my leave. Promising to return, I insisted that she keep the rest of the croissants, helped her carry the dishes to her kitchen—a small, tidy space like the rest of her living area—and then donned my coat for the trip back.

Chapter Eight

I arrived home feeling unaccountably depressed. By most measures, my visit to Bethany Probst hadn't been unpleasant. We had enjoyed some quiet time with tea and delicious croissants from Leonard's, had talked comfortably, and I gathered she seemed generally content—not nearly as unhappy as I feared she would be, nor as unhappy as I was after I left her apartment.

I decided my angst came from the issue of her children, and why, while they seemed to be the center of her universe, there was no evidence, visual at least, that they were ever in contact with her. She had not mentioned calls or visits, there were no birthday or Christmas cards on her bureau and all the photographs were older; school year pictures and snaps taken with her as a younger woman. She was an interesting character—one moment seemingly a sad old woman, the next acting sharp as could be and not in the least in need of anything. It was a mystery.

Moreover, I desperately wanted Noah *not* to be the person responsible for the fires the police were investigating. I resolved to keep my eyes peeled and my brain engaged. Perhaps I could uncover something just by being a resident on the watch.

I sat down to look at my text messages and when Rowdy wandered over, I fetched a brush and began to groom his long, fine fur. There was some Newfoundland in his background, I was quite sure—which was where the shaggy coat came from—but also some Rottweiler and who-knew-what-else. He was simply what the shelter had called him, a Big Black Dog, but with a gentleness and sweetness of nature that had made me forever his devoted slave. It was hard to imagine him as the fierce protector that had emerged last fall, but I was grateful for it.

Once his coat was shining and smooth, I moved to his nails, running a file over them and smoothing over the ends, while he lay snoring. "Rowdy!" I exclaimed, hoping to awaken him and perhaps avoid having to re-wash the kitchen rug, which would inevitably be the victim of a few spots of drool. He opened one eye, regarded me with a measure of offended dignity, and went back to sleep, which I took as a signal to give up and plan to launder the rug.

I went back to my text messages.

Things were shaping up for Saturday night. Duffy and Ashley were both 'in,' Louise was checking her calendar. It was looking like we'd have a fun get-together and possibly make some good progress on our respective quilt squares to boot. I decided to hook my computer to the television so we could watch 'Eleanor's Embroidery' as a group to get us tuned up before we dove in.

For fun, and to distract myself from thinking about Bethany Probst's odd situation, I began searching for finger-food recipes—things that were easy to eat without getting our hands, and thereby the quilt squares we were working on, covered with crumbs and smudges.

I passed a pleasant couple of hours, and as late afternoon began to creep in, I began to think about Leonard's and the promised hamburger for Rowdy. But as I was fetching his leash, the phone rang. It was Natalie.

"I've been thinking about my quilt square," she said. "What are everyone else's patterns like?"

"Mine's a street scene, Louise is doing the Burtonville water tower, and Duffy's got an old house with an unusual barn. The barn's gone. Sort of a sad story there."

"What kind of sad story?"

I cleared my throat. "A couple used to live in the house. They raised a group of foster children, but their life fell apart—I'm not sure of all the details. Now the house is dilapidated and abandoned, and the barn burned down some years ago. The woman who lived there still has a place here in Burtonville. A small apartment."

"I wonder why the house is abandoned?" asked Natalie.

"It's a big place. I expect she couldn't live there all alone. She's rather elderly. Or, at least, I think she is. I'm not actually sure how old she is."

I had a momentary recollection of my mother, who had occasionally pretended to be helpless and needy. When I accused her of pretense, she just laughed and flicked her finger on my cheek. "Who wants to help someone who acts as if they don't need it?" she commented, and laughed again.

A widow as I was, but widowed far younger, she'd gotten by on her own for years, so I guess it worked for her. She died too young, never having the chance to meet Duane or his sweet Natalie. My mother would have adored Natalie.

"But why would it become derelict?" Natalie broke into my wandering thoughts. "Seems as if they could've sold it."

I hadn't thought of that. "You're right," I said. "I'm sure there's some reason, but I don't know what it is. I'm not even sure who owns it."

"Hmm," said Natalie, and I could almost hear the gears turning, but then she said, "Oh, well. Are we on for next weekend?"

"Sounds like," I said. "Maybe not Louise, but Duffy and Ashley for sure."

"Cool," said Natalie. "I hope it's okay if I bring some books. My paper'll be turned in, but I got handed another research assignment in my methods class. I'll need to get my nose into the computer for a few hours."

"It'll be fine," I said. "If you get here early enough on Saturday, you can have several hours of quiet time before the embroidery hordes arrive."

"Embroidery hordes," snorted Natalie. "That sounds like a non sequitur."

"Hey, we embroiderers are an unruly bunch!" I protested.

"We?"

"Well, after this weekend, we'll all be experts. At least I hope," I answered.

"Me too," said Natalie. "Talk soon." And she signed off.

Rowdy was giving me his hamburger stare, so I snapped on his leash, pulled on my outdoor clothes and opened the door, but nearly jumped out of my skin when an eerie sound echoed down the street.

For a moment, I thought it was the wail that Duffy and I had heard before, and I felt gooseflesh rise on my arms, but this was different—more decidedly human, and less ghostly. Less despairing. I put my hand on Rowdy's collar, but he wasn't alarmed. Instead, he stood panting and looking up at me, then in the direction of Leonard's, no doubt wondering why we hadn't started off already.

"What was that, my man?" I asked him.

He didn't answer, of course, but he did give a fairly decisive tug on the leash in the direction of Leonard's, so I allowed him to propel me down the walk and down Beale Street toward his favorite store, even though my feet badly wanted to turn around and go home. Dusk was creeping along the snow-covered bushes, and most of the citizenry of Burtonville had returned to their homes, likely inside eating their dinners, I supposed, so the streets were mostly empty.

I wished someone would emerge and wave hello, or at least tug a garbage can out to the curb. With the snow, the world was spookily silent.

But I'd promised Rowdy his treat, so trying to ignore my growing unease, we strode along smartly, with perhaps a bit more haste than we normally exhibited on our walks. Rowdy was tugging me along, bent on hamburgers, and soon my thoughts began turning from strange sounds to the cheesy goodness of Leonard's special pizza recipe.

It was, therefore, most unwelcome when the sound came again, and a crouched figure emerged from the bushes to my left.

This time, I jumped so high I think my booted feet actually left the ground, and I gave Rowdy's leash a yank. Offended, he looked over his shoulder at me, while I put one hand on my chest and took several deep breaths, trying to get my heart rate under control.

It was Nancy Brock, her red hair stuffed under a brown knit hat. She had a large flashlight clutched in her mittened hand.

"Nancy!" I exclaimed. "Lord, you nearly gave me a stroke! What on earth are you doing?"

"Hunting for the cat," she answered. "I think I spied it about half an hour ago, but it's gone into hiding somewhere."

"Was it you making that sound?"

"What, this?" Nancy pursed her lips and made the shrieking call, nearly making me clap my hands over my ears. "I was calling for the cat."

I refrained from telling her that any self-respecting cat hearing that noise was likely to be in the next county, if not the next state. Instead, I interrupted the shrill ululation by saying, "Is it the tortie you're hunting? I think it has a home."

Nancy gave me a sharp look. "Then why's it outside?"

I felt a surge of irritation. I didn't care for this woman much. I didn't particularly like her idiosyncrasies, but I especially didn't like how they manifested themselves. She was sharp-tongued and downright mean to Bethany at the church get-together, and her social skills were decidedly lacking. Plus, if Ashley was right and she plucked up cats that weren't even hers—cats she couldn't take care of—she was probably making a lot of people unhappy. There was something very unsettling about her.

"It's an indoor-outdoor cat," I said shortly. "And I'm quite sure it belongs to Bethany Probst. You should leave it alone."

Nancy snorted. "Bethany Probst. Her son's a nasty punk and a delinquent, but don't try to tell her that. She's no prize herself."

Another wave of irritation. "I wouldn't," I snapped. "It would upset her and it isn't needed." *And what do you have against Bethany Probst?* I wasn't going to ask, but her words took me aback. *'She's no prize herself.'* What did that mean?

"Wait 'til he torches something else," Nancy shot back and turned her back on me. "Next time it might not be a pile of trash or an empty shed."

She started on up the sidewalk, shining her flashlight under the bushes, bending at the waist and pushing aside branches. At least she wasn't making that horrible cry anymore. "Nancy!" I called, but she ignored me.

I should stop her, I thought, but I wasn't sure how.

I watched her, frowning, my hand resting on patient Rowdy's head, and hoped the cat—if had been nearby—was long gone. Finally, I turned and we continued on our way. I comforted myself with the thought that something could easily be done if Bethany's cat came up missing. Nancy lived right in town, and if she had a record of grabbing random cats, it wouldn't be difficult to get someone to visit and ask if it was there. I decided to call Brad and get his take on the matter.

However, my appetite for Leonard's pizza was gone, and my bad mood had come rushing back in full force. There had been too many strange things happening in Burtonville for me to feel comfortable with people creeping around at night. And what if Nancy Brock had more on her mind than cats?

Chapter Nine

My promise to Rowdy was sacred, however, and Rowdy's appetite undiminished, so we continued on our way up the street despite my angst.

When we arrived at Leonard's, I pushed open the door with more force than was absolutely necessary. My encounter with Nancy had left me angry and confused. What was more, the wind had come up and the tips of my ears were burning from cold. So much for a warm spell. Rowdy had an open invitation to come inside the store, so long as he waited by the door. I looped his leash over a hook and wandered to the back counter where I could see Benny Leonard waiting on a customer.

I watched them curiously. The young man was buying cigarettes and a six pack of beer. He had long, blond hair pulled back in a rubber band and was wearing a leather coat that hardly looked heavy enough to protect him from the cold night. He glanced over his shoulder at me and I smiled briefly, but he didn't return the gesture. Instead, he reached for his beer and his change, and I was startled to see a long tattoo on his wrist, orange and gold, like a flame.

He picked up his items, gave me one more careless glance, and strode out away. Soon I heard the bell jangle as the door opened and closed. I raised my eyebrows and went to the counter.

"Who was that?" I asked Benny, who had spied Rowdy and was already reaching for a paper tray and some aluminum foil to wrap up a large plain hamburger.

"Him?" Benny jerked his chin at the front of the store, and I looked over my shoulder. Through the window, I could see the customer who had been at the counter now out in the parking lot, opening his car door and juggling his beer into the front seat.

I nodded.

"That's Carter Burton, Bob and Madeline's son. I haven't seen him in a while—maybe he and his parents are back on speaking terms." Benny grinned.

"Bob and Madeline Burton?"

Last fall, Bob's habit of cruising up and down in his car when he and Madeline were arguing had caused me some anxious moments. I hadn't seen him recently, but Ashley said he often went to the Prairie City truck stop when the weather turned cold and he wanted to get out of the house.

"Yeah," Benny answered. "He doesn't live around here. He had a place in Peoria. I'm not sure if he's back or what."

"Oh," I said, and suddenly felt uneasy. What was the tattoo I'd seen on his arm? Brad had called that gang the Pyros. And they were a Peoria gang. "Do you know him well?" I asked.

Benny glanced at me curiously. "Some," he answered. "Like I said, he hasn't been around for a while. Doesn't get along with Bob and Madeline. Actually, I thought he was in jail. He must be out."

I looked out the window again, but his car was gone. I shrugged, deciding I'd asked all I could. I wasn't like Ashley, who had a gift for wrestling information from even the most reluctant individuals. Benny finished wrapping up Rowdy's hamburger and dropped it into a bag. "Pizza for you?" he asked.

"Not tonight," I said. "Thanks anyway." Any appetite I'd had earlier in the day was long gone. The encounter with Nancy Brock had been upsetting enough, and now I was troubled about the young man in the store, while knowing I was probably being unreasonable. I had learned last fall that the Burton household was quarrelsome. It was unsurprising that their son was a part of the fray. But showing up out of the blue? And that tattoo? The Pyros? It was a little too much of a coincidence for me.

I paid for Rowdy's burger and started for Beale Street, Rowdy prancing along next to me with an enthusiasm reserved only for the most exciting of circumstances—and a Leonard's hamburger, of course. When we reached the blessed warmth of home, I tore the burger in two halves, fending my enthusiastic dog off with my foot, and set the snack in his bowl, leaving him to slurp it up while I shed my coat and boots.

Then I picked up my phone and called Ashley.

"Hey!" she said. "What's the news on this weekend?"

"Natalie and Duffy are both yes; Louise is still checking. But we'll go ahead with the bee," I answered. "I'm making finger foods and I'm going to show those videos."

"Duffy's coming?" Ashley sounded hesitant.

"Duffy. Yes," I answered. "He doesn't know anything about embroidery, but he can knit, so—"

"Wow," Ashley answered. "There is no way Matt would ever go to a sewing bee."

"Duffy's different," I said. "In a good way," I added, knowing—as Louise had pointed out—that much of what he did, he did for me and me alone. It was both a joy and a sorrow that I couldn't seem to give him more than my friendship. Yet? Or perhaps never? It was the perpetual question. I turned my attention back to Ashley.

"Ashley," I said. "Tell me about Nancy Brock." I had a sudden thought. "Did you tell anyone about that trash possibly being set afire deliberately?"

"What?"

"That fire in the trash can. You said Matt and the fire squad thought it might've been set by someone. I thought that information was confidential."

"It was. It is. You didn't tell anyone, did you? I shouldn't've said anything. Matt told me not to."

"I promise, I didn't," I answered. "I just wondered." *But how did Nancy know?* I thought. *Why did she think Noah set that fire?*

"You asked about Nancy?" Ashley said.

"Yes. What's she like, other than prickly and preoccupied with cats?"

"I don't know her too terribly well. I'm not sure anyone does."

"You don't?" That statement coming from Ashley was astounding enough in and of itself.

"She keeps to herself," Ashley said a bit defensively. "And when she's in groups people tend to avoid her. She's difficult and argumentative. I've heard she's a heavy drinker, but I haven't seen her drunk I don't think."

"Does she have friends in town?"

"Not many," Ashley said. "At least no one close that I know of. She has family in Peoria."

"Peoria," I said. There was a long silence.

"Why do you ask?" Ashley said.

"I just wondered. I ran into her tonight. She's got a thing about a tortie cat that she thought she saw by the Abbott house, but I think it may actually be Bethany Probst's. I wish she'd leave it alone."

"Yeah," said Ashley. "If she picks it up, the Sheriff's department'll have to go get it from her and she'll be difficult. It's a problem."

"What does she have against Bethany?" I asked. "She called Noah, Bethany's son, a delinquent—"

"Well, he sort of is," said Ashley, laughing.

"But then she said Bethany was no prize. What did she mean by that?"

Ashley hesitated. "She's probably talking about that mess when Bethany and her husband divorced and the kids were taken away. Her husband accused Bethany of neglecting the children and it turned into a real war. No one ever proved anything, although protective services interviewed them all, including the kids. It seemed sort of unbelievable to me, considering how Bethany doted on their children. I always thought maybe it was just pure meanness on her husband's part."

"Yes," I said. "Sounds as if it could be."

"I asked Joe about it at the time, but none of the Forrest foster kids were in his grade. He got to know Noah a little, but only because of his reputation. Noah was a troublemaker even back then, and he always came to school looking as if he'd been dressed from the rag bag. But it's hard to know. My son was a lot younger then."

"Sounds as if Nancy's got a grudge against Bethany for some reason," I commented.

"Maybe. But she's basically got a grudge against everyone."

"Seems like," I said. "How about Carter Burton? Do you know him?"

"That's a name I haven't heard in a while. How'd you meet him?"

"I ran into him at Leonard's."

"Leonard's? I didn't know he ever came to Burtonville."

"Apparently he does now."

"I thought he was long gone. Hated it here. Lived in Peoria for a while. Went to jail for embezzling. Strange that he's turning up now."

"That's sort of what I thought," I said, frowning.

The conversation turned to the weekend and embroidering and, inevitably, to food. Ashley volunteered to bring puff pastry and an array of homemade jams, and again exclaimed over Duffy's coming. Was there anything he particularly liked to eat?

"He eats everything. Just treat him like one of the crowd." I grinned.

"Okay," said Ashley doubtfully. "But if Matt were there'd want steak or something."

"Duffy eats everything," I repeated, and Ashley said, "Huh," which made me laugh.

We signed off and I went to the computer to look up a recipe for slow cooker hot chocolate. Somehow the idea of an always-warm vat of chocolatey goodness seemed just what the party needed. I found myself staring at my favorite photo of Duane and me—the one that always sat by on my desk.

What would you think of all this? I asked him. *All the drama and undercurrents in this little town?* My husband had always been so practical and nothing people did ever surprised him. I wanted him to talk to. He would know what to make of all these personalities.

Carter Burton seemed to hold a grudge against Burtonville. Could he be our firebug?

Nancy Brock had issues, but I wasn't sure whether it was fair to include arson. I wished she weren't so nasty.

I also wished I could forget her words. *Wait 'til Noah torches something else. Next time, it might not be a pile of trash.*

Chapter Ten

Natalie arrived on Saturday morning in a swirl of snow, falling on Rowdy with a glad squeal and then hugging me tightly in greeting.

"Mummy!" she cried. "How are you?"

"Good! Particularly good, now," I replied, kissing her on the forehead. "It's great to see you, honey."

I helped her lug her suitcase into the den, and she threw herself onto the bed. "I'm tempted to take a nap," she said, "but I have to get a little work done on this research report. Mind if I hide out in here for a while?"

"Not at all," I said. "Shall I shut Rowdy out?"

"Nooo!" Natalie protested. "He's my inspiration."

"For a psychology research report?" I replied. "That's rather scary. And here I thought he was a simple soul."

"Rowdy? Simple? Perish the thought!" Natalie's hazel eyes twinkled at me. She opened her computer case and pulled out her laptop, setting it carefully on the desk. "C'mon over here, Rowdy. She just doesn't understand you."

I smiled and left the two of them alone, Natalie's dark head bent over her keyboard and Rowdy asleep, as usual, his big jaws resting on her foot. I hoped her shoes were drool-proof.

Out in the kitchen, I measured cocoa powder, semi-sweet chocolate chips, and sugar into my slow cooker in preparation for the evening's festivities, then began the task of making finger sandwiches. I'd bought a loaf of Leonard's best mixed grain bread, and made egg salad and tuna sandwiches, then added cucumber sandwiches with fresh herbed cream cheese to the tray, thinking of Duffy. Yes, he ate everything, but he especially liked cucumber sandwiches.

To my delight, Louise texted me, **Sorry for the late notice. I lied to my poetry group and said I had a date, so I'll be there tonight!**

They let u go on a date? I texted back.

Occasionally, she answered. **Hence, the lie!**

I grinned. Louise taught and studied tragic poetry, and her colleagues weren't sure there was anything to life beyond their scholarship. Louise occasionally had to take drastic actions to escape.

As I cut sandwiches and arranged them on the tray, my thoughts turned again to the spate of fires in Burtonville. Set deliberately or accidents? If deliberately, set by whom and for what reason? Was it the Pyros, enacting their initiation rites as Brad Stanton suspected, or something different? I scratched my head, reached for my coffee cup, discovered it was empty, and decided the universe was giving me a message to take a break.

I wandered into the living room and found Natalie had already abandoned her paper. She and Rowdy were curled on the rug and she was carefully painting Rowdy's toenails fire engine red.

I grinned. "He prefers pink."

Natalie sighed. "I know, but I left his favorite shade back at my apartment. This'll have to do."

I glanced at Rowdy, who was snoring gently. "It doesn't seem to be causing him any mental distress. And the red does show up nicely against the black."

"That's what I thought," Natalie commented, lifting one of Rowdy's paws to inspect her handiwork. Predictably, Rowdy didn't bother to open his eyes.

"Want some coffee?" I asked.

"Sure thing," Natalie said. "I'll be done in a minute. You got any flavored creamers?"

"A whole array." I turned and went into the kitchen, put out two mugs and three different creamer choices and started the coffee pot brewing.

In a couple of minutes, Natalie strode in and picked up a mug. "This is such fun," she said. "Just like the old days with everyone coming over. I hope I don't make a mess of my quilt square."

"We're all in the same boat," I reassured her. "No one's done any embroidery lately, and some of us not in years. Some of us never. We'll help each other out, and the videos will be good."

“Yeah,” said Natalie. She poured herself coffee, inspected the creamer choices, and selected caramel mocha. Then she sat down at the table across from me. “You look as if you want to talk.”

I smiled. “Something’s on my mind, and I thought maybe I could ask you before the gang arrives.”

“Uh oh.”

“It’s nothing bad. I just want to pick your psychological brain.”

“Oh, that!” Natalie grinned. “Let me get ready.” She sat back in her chair, crossed her legs, and stroked an imaginary beard. “Now, Frau Reed, what seems to be the trouble?”

“Ha ha,” I said wryly but grinned back at her. “What do you know about people who start fires?”

“Start fires!” Natalie exclaimed. “Like arson?” She leaned forward in her chair. “Don’t tell me you’re in the midst of another mystery! I thought you got that all out of your system last fall.”

“Not me personally,” I said. “But Burtonville. There have been several rather odd situations recently, revolving around fires. It’s been on my mind.”

“Are you talking about people who set fires to hurt someone?”

I thought back to the recent occurrences. A pile of trash, an old shed by an empty home. “I don’t think so,” I answered. “The police are trying not to alarm anyone,” I said. “But Ashley told me—“

“Naturally,” interrupted Natalie.

I smiled. "Ashley's a gossip, but she isn't malicious. And I think she picks her audience. She knows I don't spread rumors and I wouldn't deliberately alarm people. Besides, Brad Stanton told me about it, too. They suspect the fires might have been deliberately set."

"Brad Stanton?" asked Natalie, and wiggled her eyebrows.

"Never mind that," I said firmly. "Back to my original question. What kind of people light fires deliberately?"

"Hmm. That's a really broad question. There's criminal behavior and then there are people with mental illness. We're not talking insurance fraud or something, right?"

"Don't think so."

"Okay. Then let's focus on people who feel compelled to light fires."

"Brad said they suspect a gang. Out of Peoria."

"Well, I'd say gang violence would usually fall into the category of criminal behavior. Gangs induce a sense of belonging. But there are group dynamics and pressure to fit in. Threats, too. You know, 'You joined us; now you gotta do this or else.' That kind of stuff."

"I get that," I said. "What else?"

"Well, if we're ruling out criminal arson, or a deliberate attempt to kill or injure someone, then an individual with a disturbed mind or a problem with impulse control might start fires. Either of those could also come into play with a person who commits criminal arson or wants to harm someone else, of course."

"Okay." I put my chin in my hand. "I don't know where all this is heading. I've just been thinking, you know."

"Ooh, thinking! *Very* dangerous!" commented Natalie.

I smiled. "Yeah. I'm probably too involved, but there's just weird stuff happening. Like this woman keeps showing up at odd moments. She's got odd fixations, and she's awkward and occasionally belligerent socially. The police are focused on this gang, but I keep wondering if there's more to the story. Frankly, I wonder if it's got anything to do with the gang at all."

"Who is the woman you're talking about?"

"She lives here in Burtonville. I met her at the quilt kick-off at the church, and she sort of struck me the wrong way. She's obsessed with cats, too."

Natalie grinned. "Sounds like someone after my own heart."

"Um. No," I said. "She's nothing like you. Then there's a man. Son of a couple who lived here. He hasn't been around for a while, and now he's showing up like a bad penny. Has been in jail, but not for fire-starting."

Natalie sipped her coffee. "What's the gang?"

"They're called the Pyros," I answered. "They have a chapter or a guild, or whatever you call it, over in Peoria. Brad said their initiation is to set fires. One of the gang members has some connections to Burtonville from quite a few years ago, and I guess that's part of the deal. Burn up your roots or something?"

"Scary," said Natalie.

"Really. Although up to now, it's just been some old trash and a shed next to a house where no one lives—at least not yet. It's that big old house across the street. The one with the gables. It's sold, but the new owners haven't moved in yet."

"Hmm ... two fires? Could be a coincidence. That isn't exactly a huge number."

"I agree, but the police are taking it seriously and the shed was a pretty big fire. It could have been much more serious, and I have the feeling they know things they aren't necessarily sharing. Brad implied as much."

"People who have a mood disorder and light fires do it because they need to relieve some sort of tension or to induce a sense of calm, interestingly enough. Some have an unhealthy fascination with fire. Sometimes they have substance abuse problems, too."

I looked up quickly. "Substance abuse?"

Natalie wrinkled her forehead. "Yeah, drugs or alcohol or something. Often they have a big build-up of stress that they can't relieve, and somehow lighting a fire releases the pressure. But people who light fires are often pretty seriously mentally ill. They usually have a lot of problems."

"Substance abuse," I echoed. I harkened back to my conversation with Ashley about Nancy

Brock. *I've heard she's a heavy drinker*, Ashley had said.

"Where does the woman live?" Natalie asked, recognizing, in the odd way she had, the direction my thoughts had taken.

"Maybe six blocks from here," I said. "Over across from the church."

Natalie sat quietly, gazing at me, and I studied my coffee cup. I really didn't care for Nancy. I went down my list of complaints one more time. She had made me uncomfortable at the church, I didn't like the idea of her nabbing people's pets and I didn't like her attitude toward Bethany Probst. It was rather startling to recognize the depth of my antipathy toward her. It was unsettling and made me feel ashamed. People with drinking problems and a fixation about cats weren't necessarily arsonists. Time to put Nancy Brock out of my mind. But I hadn't given up on the idea that it was possible the police were on the wrong track. Maybe Noah was a troublemaker, but did that necessarily make him the arsonist?

"Everything okay?" Natalie asked, and I jerked myself out of my reverie.

"Yes," I said and stood up. "Life is a bit annoying at the moment."

"Not again?" Natalie asked. "I really hoped you were past all that, after the robbery."

"This is a little different. But let's not dwell on it. We've got a night of fun ahead of us, and we should get ourselves in the mood. Let's start the hot chocolate. No harm in getting it going a little early."

"To getting ourselves in the mood," said my stepdaughter, raising her coffee mug in a toast, and she got up to help me finish the food preparations for our embroidery bee.

Chapter Eleven

Ashley arrived at 2 PM, carrying a big tray of pastries, six decorative pots filled with different flavors of jams and jellies, and even some apple butter. By that time, the cocoa had begun to fill the house with its delicious aroma, and we decided the three of us ought to sample it. So we sat at the table, smiling and content, sipping gingerly at the hot liquid and nibbling sugar cookies.

Soon Louise drove in, followed closely by Duffy, who brought two bottles of wine and a bowl of mixed fruit.

"Nice toes, buddy," Duffy said to Rowdy, who was sprawled on the living room carpet. "But do you think red's his color?"

"Today it is," said Natalie. "I could do yours, too."

Duffy inspected his fingernails with interest. "Think it goes with my sweater?"

I laughed.

In a matter of minutes, everyone had fetched mugs and was sitting around the living room, munching on finger sandwiches and pastries, exclaiming over Louise's crab dip, and sipping their cocoa, Duffy's mug piled high with marshmallows. Quilt squares and an array of embroidery floss littered the floor, and I queued up 'Eleanor's Embroidery Excellence' to get us in the mood.

"We need more cocoa," announced Natalie, her mouth full of crab dip, and Ashley followed me into the kitchen to help restock.

Silence fell in the living room, and while we added more ingredients to the slow cooker, Ashley chattered away about her quilt block, about her husband and son, and about the secret garden she and I planned to create in my side yard next spring.

"Mums, definitely," she said resolutely, grabbing a tray and setting out some clean mugs. "Some herbs and maybe daisies or Black-Eyed Susans. It'll be beautiful, you'll see."

A movement out in the yard caught my eye and I glanced out the window into the gathering dark. All was still. I craned my neck toward the cornfield. "It needs to be an easy-care garden, though," I commented. "Are all those things easy-care? You've never seen how quickly I can kill a plant."

"No problem!" Ashley said over her shoulder as she strode toward the living room with the tray. "The secret is tons of mulch." A few moments later, she was back.

"What are you doing?" she asked, joining me by the stove.

"Looking out the window," I answered. "I could have sworn ..."

"Sworn what?"

"I thought I saw someone out there. A person walking through the snow. By the cornfield."

"In this weather?" Ashley said. "They'd have to be crazy."

Who was crazier than Nancy Brock? I had a momentary impulse to charge out into the yard and confront her, but I remembered my stern advice to myself to stop obsessing about Nancy, and I turned away from the window.

"Never mind," I said. "I probably imagined it. Let's put this food together and get going on the–"

Ashley interrupted me by leaning close and whispering, "They're all reading."

"What? Who?" I asked.

"Louise and Duffy and Natalie." Ashley looked over her shoulder as if worried she'd be overheard.

I looked toward the living room. It was definitely very quiet out where my friends were gathered. "Reading?"

"Yes. No one's even looking at the quilting supplies."

I smiled. "I'll handle this," I said. I cast one last look at the cornfield and marched toward the living room. For right now, I had to rouse my guests and put the spirit of embroidery back into their souls. Besides, I didn't want to alarm anyone, and it was possible I'd imagined seeing anything at all out there. I strode into the living room.

There was Natalie, lying on the rug with Rowdy curled against her, scanning the American Psychological Association website. Louise had her nose in The Tragic Poetry of Emily Dickinson, while Duffy was lost behind The New York Times.

"Guys!" I said loudly. Rowdy twitched one ear. "Are you getting yourselves psyched up for embroidering? I'm sensing some avoidance behavior here."

Louise stuffed her paperback book into her purse. "Of course we are," she said. "We just need more food, and then we're good to go."

Duffy folded down the corner of the paper and looked at me over his glasses, and Natalie just grinned.

"Okay," I said. "I'm pressing *Go* on the video." Then, "Ashley!" I called. "Bring in the sandwiches before we lose them again!"

"Coming," she answered, and I clicked to begin 'Eleanor's Embroidery.'

We watched two of her instructional sessions, one on getting started and one called 'Art of Embroidery.' The techniques Eleanor discussed had me lost in moments, but Duffy and Louise were paying close attention, so I kept it running, trying to absorb as much as I could, and took a poll when the episode had finished.

"Shall we begin our own pieces?" I asked, trying to ignore the sinking feeling in my stomach when I inspected my quilt square. I wished I had selected an easier pattern. Perhaps I could buy Ashley's window box from her. I stole a look at Ashley, but she was looking askance at her pattern, too, so perhaps she had the same misgivings as I.

Despite what I detected as general apprehension, the group pronounced themselves ready, and after I went to get more food—with a stern look at everyone *not* to get distracted again by unrelated reading—we sat down with our embroidery hoops in our laps and began sewing. Soon, I had a corner of my street scene begun and had started the outline of on an old car.

I inspected the group. Natalie was biting the corner of her lip and I saw Louise picking out some stitches, but Ashley and Duffy were working quietly, and I tried not to be dispirited by the fact that my car seemed to have a perpetual flat tire, no matter how many times I re-stitched the rim. Annoyed, I set the embroidery frame down in my lap and started up 'Art of Embroidery' for a break. Duffy joined me on the couch.

"How's yours coming?" I whispered as Eleanor led us through how to make one of her gorgeous pieces.

"I dunno," answered Duffy. "Slow going."

"Yeah, me too. We have 'til March 15th, though. I've got some of mine done. I think I can finish it."

I glanced at Louise, who was picking out threads again. Natalie eyed her square, turned it upside down and then right side up again, and frowned. Not a good sign.

"More food anyone?" I asked brightly, when Eleanor finished her tutorial, making the embroidery process look maddeningly simple, when it wasn't, of course.

"Not for me," said Natalie.

"Nor I," said Louise and Ashley simultaneously.

Duffy looked at me. "More cucumber sandwiches?" I asked, and he nodded. "Okay." I got up from the couch and set my embroidery hoop on the arm. "When I get back, maybe we can take a break, have a glass of wine, and do show and tell."

"Arg," said Natalie.

"Courage!" said Louise.

Ashley looked up, grinning. "Mine's doing okay. I got the nasturtiums done. Next, I need to do forget-me-nots, which shouldn't be too hard since they'll really be just small knots."

"Show and tell when we get back," I said and left, Duffy trailing along behind me.

"I really don't need any more sandwiches," Duffy commented while he uncorked the wine.

I set five wine glasses on the table. "It's okay. I know you like them, and I've already got the herbed cream cheese made."

I took a moment to gaze out at the cornfield and Duffy asked, "What's up?"

"Probably nothing," I answered. "Just me being paranoid." In fact, I could see nothing out the window so perhaps I had been imagining things, indeed.

I laid his sandwiches in a napkin and we went back to the living room, Duffy carrying glasses and the bottle of wine. He poured some in each glass, handed them around, and raised his.

"To us!" he pronounced, to which we all solemnly replied, "To us!" and sipped.

"To the quilt!" Ashley crowed and, "To the quilt," we echoed.

"Are we showing our blocks now?" Natalie asked mournfully.

Louise looked at her watch. "We better do a status check, or else we'll be here all night."

"I agree," I said. "We should at least figure out whether we need to schedule another get-together to support each other, or if we have to call in reinforcements."

"Here's mine," said Louise, and held up her hoop. Her water tower was only partway outlined, and none of the grass or trees had been filled in. "I had to pull a lot of it out and start over," she said, staring down at it. "I think I'm getting the hang of it, though."

"And mine," said Natalie, displaying her hoop.

"Hey! Not bad!" I said. Natalie was embroidering the Burtonville bakery, and she had a nice start on the baked goods in the window, even adding a little bit of embellishment on some of the loaves of bread.

Ashley and I held up ours. My antique car still had a flat tire, but I'd decided to give up on it and move on. Ashley's window boxes were making good progress, although she needed to fill in the woodgrains on the box, and I didn't envy her that.

Duffy sighed. "C'mon, Duffy," I coaxed. "Fair's fair."

"But it's just started," he protested. "I've only done part of the barn."

"We're all in the same boat," Louise commented.

"Yeah," said Natalie.

So Duffy reached for his quilt block and held it up, and there was a long, long silence in the room. Duffy glanced worriedly at all our faces.

Finally, "I quit," said Louise, throwing her hoop into her lap.

"Me too," said Natalie, while Ashley just gazed at the scrap of fabric Duffy held in his hand.

"Hey!" he said, coloring. "I've never done this before. I didn't understand how to layer–"

"Stop, Duffy!" I cried. "That's perfectly beautiful! It's better than Eleanor's best." I stood and walked over. "Let me see it closer."

I took the hoop out of his hand and stared down at his work, at the short overlapping stitches framing the old barn, how he'd shaded the stones and captured just what that unique structure must have looked like, even though it was no longer there. In the background, the drawing of the big house stood, waiting to be stitched into existence.

Inexplicably, I felt tears threaten. That old house, now so ramshackle, when it had once been bursting with children that I hoped had been happy there. And the barn, a unique architectural structure now lost to time and the harsh reality of leaping flames. What had really happened there to bring Bethany Probst's life crashing down around her?

To cover my stab of emotion, I turned to the others. "A round of applause for Duffy," I said, and they all dutifully clapped, although Natalie was watching me closely in that intuitive way she had.

"You guys aren't really quitting, are you?" asked Duffy anxiously.

"No, they aren't quitting," I reassured him before anyone else could speak up. "They're just jealous."

"Yeah. Jealous," said Louise darkly, and took a sip of her wine.

"I think I'm getting carpal tunnel," announced Ashley, flexing her hand. "My wrist is aching."

"I think I'm getting everything-ache," added Natalie, rubbing her neck. "I vote we hang it up for tonight and schedule another bee."

"Good by me," said Louise.

"And me!" Ashley said.

"I was just getting started," Duffy began. "But that's okay. I'm okay to quit," he added when he detected several chilly looks directed his way.

"Great!" I said brightly before my guests could come to blows. "Let's finish the night just being social." Four pairs of eyes turned in my direction. "More wine, anyone?"

Chapter Twelve

We finished the second bottle of wine and I helped Duffy pack up the telescope. Then Ashley held the door while we maneuvered it outside and into the trunk of his car, covering the delicate equipment carefully with a quilt and setting the folded tripod in next to it.

Duffy stared down at the scope and touched the dark metal with one fingertip. "I'd like to borrow it again," he said. "Maybe try to find some deep sky objects or something."

"That'd be fun," I answered.

"Maybe Brad would like to join us," Duffy went on, and I glanced at him, startled, remembering how Brad had admired the telescope. Brad and Duffy and I and a buddy of Brad's had enjoyed an evening over the euchre table a month ago, and Brad and Duffy had hit it off famously. Was I the only one who found the situation somewhat strained? Neither of the men seemed to notice anything.

I sighed. "Maybe. I'll ask him."

Duffy shut his trunk. “Coffee?”

“All ready to go,” I said.

So the embroiders sat in the living room sipping coffee and the dregs of the hot chocolate, three of us staring with disfavor at the quilt squares on the coffee table. But Ashley was her usual cheerful self, and Duffy actually looked eager to get back to his. He even picked it up once or twice and ran a fingertip over his careful stitches.

“I think the quilt is going to turn out really nicely,” commented Ashley. “I can’t wait ‘til we can see it all assembled.”

“I agree,” said Louise. “Is there an unveiling or something?”

“I think the mayor is planning a picnic once the weather warms up, with some sort of celebration. Mandy Patterson, the township clerk—you met her at the church, remember?—is going to do the quilting. She’s pretty experienced.”

“Fun,” said Natalie. Then she yawned, stretching her arms high above her head. “Whew, I’m tired. I think I’ll turn in for the night. Sorry to be a party poop.”

“You go get your beauty sleep,” said Louise.

“I should go, too,” added Ashley. “This was really a fun evening. I’m not sure we need it for the quilt, but it’d be fun to get together again.”

“You got it,” I said, smiling.

Soon the rest of my guests were gathering their embroidery paraphernalia and donning outdoor gear, and Natalie stumbled toward the bedroom, Rowdy at her heels. I grabbed my coat and followed the group outside, crossing my arms across my chest as the cool night air filled my lungs.

"'Night!" called Ashley, heading off down the sidewalk, and I waved.

Then Louise backed her car out of the driveway, and she gave a short beep as she headed off down Beale Street, leaving Duffy and me to stand under the clear night sky.

"Going to be another cold one," he said.

"Yes." I sighed.

"What's the matter? Embroidery got you down?" Duffy smiled.

"No, it's not that," I said. "I'm uneasy about something. Just can't shake the feeling."

"What about?"

"Oh, it's a long story," I said.

"Go ahead."

I smiled and looked up at him. At his rumpled hair and glasses, the troubled expression on his face. "It's just that there's this woman who lives in an apartment not far from here, and I can't stop thinking about her. She's had a tough time, and she seems sort of lonely, or isolated anyway. I'm sort of worried about her. Not for any particular reason," I went on, when Duffy's forehead furrowed. "She's not sick that I know of, or in danger or anything. It's just that her son might be in trouble—in trouble *again*, that is. And I'm afraid if it's true it's really going to upset her. Then there's this other woman who doesn't like her and seems to be sort of picking on her for no reason I can think of."

"*Picking* on her?"

I grimaced. "It's complicated. She reminds me of someone—my mom or my grandmother."

"Who does? The nice woman or the evil one?"

That made me laugh. "The nice one. It's silly, really. Somehow being around her has brought back some old memories of my family, and I feel really protective toward her. If anything bad happens, it's going to make me upset."

"It's not a police matter?"

"Oh, not at all. She's not at risk of anything except more sadness, and that makes me sad."

Duffy set his hand gently on my head, and I could almost feel the warmth through his glove. "I hate to see you blue," he said. There was a short pause. "I'll call you tomorrow. Maybe things will look brighter then."

"Maybe," I answered. "Thanks for coming. And for being a good sport."

"Thanks for having me," he said. With a last quick stroke of my hair, he folded his tall frame into his car and headed off down the road.

I made my way inside, inspected the dirty dishes in the sink, and decided to leave them for tomorrow. Natalie and Rowdy seemed down for the count, and the house felt empty, suddenly. Was Bethany Probst asleep and dreaming? Or was she sitting and reading, alone in her small living room?

I sighed again and prepared to go to bed, feeling more awake than I wished I was. I climbed under the covers and gave my pillow a shake, trying to think about something different.

But it was no use. I wasn't sleepy at all, and now my brain was going a hundred miles an hour. The fires. It was Noah. It had to be Noah. Brad Stanton had all but said it was Noah. But what if it wasn't Noah? The narrow, sullen face of Nancy Brock appeared in my head like a specter. *Stop it,* I told myself sternly.

But she moved here from Peoria, my brain stubbornly replied.

Be quiet, I told my brain.

And what about that other young man? The Burtons' son?

Are you suspecting anyone who has a tattoo now? I answered my brain nastily.

Why not? asked my brain.

I sat up in bed and put my hands on top of my head. Apparently, sleep was going to elude me for a while. I sat there for a moment, and once I felt I'd managed to stem the tide of conversation in my head, I turned on my bedside lamp, snagged my glasses, and felt around next to the bed for the paperback I'd been reading. I opened it and settled back against my pillow.

But, minutes later, I had let the book fall down against the quilt and found myself staring out into the darkness, imagining flames clawing the heavens and figures wreathed in smoke. I wasn't necessarily a faithful subscriber to hunches, as was Brad Stanton, but I believed one ignored gut feelings at one's peril.

And I didn't like what my gut was telling me.

Chapter Thirteen

When I finally staggered out of bed the next morning, I found Natalie already up and making coffee, and Rowdy out in the yard taking care of his morning business.

“Good morning!” Natalie sang, and I gave her a look through slitted eyes. “Wow, what happened to you?” she went on.

“Couldn’t sleep,” I croaked, reaching for the coffee pot. I felt miserable, my head aching and a gritty feeling under my eyelids. I wondered if I might be getting a cold. “I lay in bed thinking for the longest time, and then when I did go to sleep I had a bunch of weird dreams. Never mind. Maybe I’ll take a nap later today.”

“I thought I’d head home after lunch,” Natalie said. “Do a little work here, and then get back before it’s dark.”

I took a sip of coffee, and it felt wonderful on my throat. There was definitely a cold lurking somewhere. I hoped I could fight it off. “Are you using this?" I asked, pointing at Natalie's laptop, which was sitting on the kitchen table.

"Not right now," she said and pushed it in my direction. "What're you looking for?" She sat down next to me and put her chin in her hand, then got up when she heard Rowdy at the door.

Rowdy lumbered into the kitchen, his long hair tipped in snow. He came and put his head in my lap and I yelped when his icy nose pressed against my wrist. Pushing him gently away and scratching his ear with one hand, I moused over to a browser window and typed in a search string.

"What're you looking for?" Natalie repeated.

"*Peoria News*," I answered. "I want to see if I can find ... Ah, yes. Here." I pointed at the screen.

Gang Violence Blamed for Warehouse Fire

"More on the fire problem?" Natalie asked.

"I was just curious. Wondering about the gang thing."

Natalie's eyes skimmed over the search results. She pointed. "There's another one, more recent."

Police Investigate Alley Fire

I clicked. It was dated three days before. There had been a fire in a dumpster that spread rapidly to trash and debris strewn in a back street. A small apartment building had been evacuated and a woman treated for smoke inhalation.

Rowdy groaned, and I looked down at him. "He's ready for breakfast. Natalie, search on Pyros, would you?"

"Pyros?" Natalie pulled the laptop over in front of her and as I got up to fetch Rowdy's bowl I heard her fingers flying over the keys. "Okay, here's something."

I dumped Rowdy's food into his bowl and added warm water. "Would you read it to me?"

"The street gang Pyro and its rival, F1100, continue to be investigated by local police for possible involvement in half a dozen suspicious fires over the past month," Natalie read. "Originally part of the same gang (F1100), the Pyros split off to form a separate band—using violence, threats of violence, and arson to protect their turf, sell drugs and initiate new members. F1100 (the name derives from the temperature of a lit fire, 1,100 degrees Fahrenheit), cooperated with police to investigate several drug deals involving rival gangs on their turf. That action, seen as undesirable cooperation with law enforcement, caused some F1100 members to cleave away from the original gang to form the Pyros." She paused. "Want me to go on?"

I set Rowdy's bowl on the floor. "Is there anything about Noah?"

"Noah who?"

"Noah ..." I thought for a moment, realizing I didn't know his surname. "I guess I don't have the last name. He was a foster child of Bethany Probst."

"There might be articles from when he went to school here. When did he graduate?"

"I'm not sure he did. He's a few years older than Ashley's son, Joe. Ashley would know when or if he graduated. But ... never mind. It's not that important." I gazed out my kitchen window and something caught my eye. "All right, that's it!" I exclaimed.

Along the perimeter of my yard, next to the cornfield that backed up to Rowdy's invisible fence, a trail of footprints led through the snow.

Natalie looked up from her computer. "What?" she said.

"Someone's been out in my yard."

Natalie joined me at the window. "Not again! Last fall…"

"This is different," I said grimly, forgetting all about my vow, or perhaps choosing to ignore it. "I'm positive I know who it is."

Natalie wrinkled her forehead. "Who?"

"It's that Nancy Brock."

"Nancy …?"

"Nancy Brock. The woman with the weird cat fixation. She's been here stalking Bethany Probst's cat. I thought I saw someone in my yard last night, but I didn't want to break up the party."

"Last night …?" echoed Natalie.

"Last night," I repeated. "I'm going to call Brad Stanton." I strode out into the living room, feeling as if anger radiated out of my very pores. In the reasonable part of my mind, I knew lack of sleep and my still-nagging headache was contributing to this spurt of rage, but I didn't care.

Natalie came running behind me. "Wait," she said. "What's going on?"

"Where's my phone?" I snarled.

"I dunno. In your bedroom?"

I hurried into the bedroom, grabbed my phone off the bedside stand, and phoned Brad. Fortunately, I got his voicemail. Fortunately, because I was angry and not at my most coherent. Also fortunately, because almost as soon as I made the call, I had second thoughts.

I had a split second to pull myself together and I mostly managed it. "Would you give me a ring, Brad? I want to ask you a question. Thanks," I said, in what I hoped was a modulated tone of voice. I hoped my annoyance wouldn't be obvious in my message.

"Mummy, I don't think those footprints are in your yard," Natalie called. "It seems as if they're in the cornfield, actually."

"What?" I clicked my phone off and went back to the window where Natalie was still staring outside.

She turned and looked at me. "I don't think anyone was in your yard," she repeated. "I can see footprints in the cornfield, though."

I went to the window and stared out, narrowing my eyes. Natalie was right. The line of footprints actually went past my property and out into the cornfield. Why anyone would be out there was a mystery, but I supposed it could have been anyone. The night of the Abbott shed fire, it seemed as if most of the residents of Burtonville had been out wandering around, quite probably in the cornfield. And after all, the cornfield wasn't part of my property—perhaps the owners were out there for something or other.

I'd be less suspicious if I hadn't had that experience last fall, I thought. And perhaps I needed to get more accustomed to life in a small town. In Peoria, no one went walking through someone else's yard; in Burtonville, things were much looser. I needed to stop being so paranoid.

I sighed and turned to look at my stepdaughter, struck suddenly by how much she resembled her mother, Iris, with her long dark hair and hazel eyes. Natalie looked concerned, but not alarmed, and she would be heading back to her apartment and school in just a couple of hours. I could explore unwelcome visitors later. For now, I wanted to enjoy my stepdaughter.

By all accounts, Iris had been a sensible and level-headed person and, not for the first time, I wondered what had attracted Duane to me. I was far from sensible when I got a head of steam going; yet, Duane and I had a satisfying and successful marriage.

I asked him once, *What on earth do you see in me, Duane?* after a particularly tempestuous day, but he had only smiled and kissed my hand. *All the things*, he answered. It was a sweet memory.

So, for the sake of Natalie's father, whom I had adored, and in the interest of preserving the remainder of what had been a delightful weekend, I let the curtain fall back into place and turned to his daughter.

"I'm imagining things again, my dear. Let's make the most of this day. What sounds like fun?"

"Pancakes?"

“Okay, then,” I said, and went to assemble the makings, resolutely ignoring my swirling thoughts of lonely and troubled women, alienated and disenfranchised young people, roaring flames, wandering cats, and my lost husband, who would have held my hands and made me feel better.

Chapter Fourteen

Natalie and I passed a pleasant morning stuffing ourselves on pancakes, coloring one of her impossibly-difficult mandala coloring pages, and chatting about her school program, her love life and her internship.

"I'm afraid I'm going to be super busy for the next few weeks," she said. "I've got to squash in twenty hours a week of internship time on top of my courses. It'll mean I may not be able to come visit quite so often."

"I'll miss you," I said sincerely. "I'll make a trip over on spring break."

"That would be nice. I'd like you to meet Robert. If we're still going out, that is. He's nice. Engineering major. Depressingly smart."

I grinned. "I'd like that."

After lunch, Rowdy and I stood at the door watching her drive away and I scratched Rowdy behind the ears when he let out a small whine. "We won't be able to stay at her apartment if you go along, my man." Rowdy looked up at me, panting.

"We'll have to find a hotel that takes dogs." Rowdy's stare didn't waver. "Don't look so insistent," I added. "Yes, you're going."

At that, Rowdy padded away to collapse onto the living room rug, and within moments he was snoring loudly.

I watched him, yawning. Even the multiple cups of coffee I'd consumed with Natalie hadn't revived me completely after my disturbed night. I nodded. "Good strategy. Think I'll take a nap too."

I wandered into the bedroom and pulled the quilt up over my legs. It took less than a minute for me to be as sound asleep as my dog. Out in the living room, my cell phone rang and then rang again. Brad Stanton returned my call, I discovered later, but my phone was muted, and I never heard a thing.

Instead, I slept long and hard and soundly, footprints in the snow far from my mind.

I got up at twilight and let Rowdy outside. It was a spectacular evening, clear and cold, with an orange and pink sunset blazing over the trees and most of Burtonville apparently tucked in for the night.

Soup seemed as if it should be on the menu, so I dug out a can of my favorite chicken noodle and some garlic bread, let Rowdy inside and prepared his dinner. Outside, shadows crept across the lawn and a sliver of moon began to rise above the cornfield. A good night for stargazing if we'd still had the telescope.

On the other hand, I was happy for a quiet evening inside, so I fetched my glasses and my paperback, brewed a cup of tea, and curled up on the couch, Rowdy snoring at my feet. My reading selection was a biography of *Oscar Wilde*. Louise would have approved.

I was deeply engrossed in chapter four when an explosion of pounding on my front door made me jump and grab at my teacup to prevent it spilling all over the floor. Rowdy raised his head and stared at the door, and I vaulted over the top of him to get to the window and see who was knocking.

It was Ashley. I threw open the door and she nearly fell inside, panting and holding a hand up to her chest. "Marianne!" she exclaimed. "Leonard's is on fire! Is your phone turned off?"

I reached automatically for my jeans pocket and my cell phone, but it wasn't there. I looked past her and saw a plume of smoke. "Leonard's is on fire?" I echoed. "What—?"

And then I heard the distant scream of sirens heading from Prairie City.

"There are two houses in danger," Ashley gasped. "We're trying to get the people and their valuables out, just in case. Can you help? There are three dogs there that need somewhere to go."

"I'll help," I said quickly. "You stay here," I told Rowdy, who had finally clambered to his feet. "We may have company."

I shoved my feet into my boots, grabbed my coat and mittens, and sprinted off down the street after Ashley, who was already half a block ahead of me. There were shouts and calls coming from the direction of Leonard's, but we headed straight for a tall, gabled house with a line of people at the front door. They had formed a bucket brigade and were handing household items out into the snow, lugging them down the block and setting them as carefully as possible in a neighboring garage.

"Our photographs!" cried a panicky voice, and I saw a forty-something woman rush back into the house.

I followed her. "Hand them to me," I called, and took a pile of leather-bound albums out of her hands, carrying them past the people moving furniture and setting them alongside a pile of file folders in the garage where other items were gathering.

I saw Ashley hurrying down the block and I ran up next to her. "Where are the dogs?"

"Over there!" She pointed, and I saw a Dalmatian and two smaller dogs of questionable breed. A crying boy of maybe eight or nine had his arms around the Dalmatian. The two little dogs were tied to a tree and barking frantically.

Behind me, two fire engines had screeched to a halt and firefighters poured out, dragging hoses. I ran over to the boy and crouched next to him. "Is this your dog?"

"Y-yes-sss!" He was crying so hard he could hardly speak.

"Where are your mom and dad?"

"My mom's back at the house. She said to stay with Barney. But I'm scared."

"Are the other dogs yours, too?"

"No, they're the neighbors' dogs. Is my house going to burn down?"

"I don't think so," I answered, having no real idea. A woman ran up.

"Are you okay, Donald?" she asked, glancing at me.

"I'm Marianne Reed from over on Beale Street," I said quickly. "Can I take Barney, at least, to my house? I can take the other two dogs, too, but ..."

"The owners aren't here," said the woman breathlessly. "We were house-sitting for them—" She broke off, as a tower of flames shot up into the sky. "Oh God," she gasped.

"Let me take the dogs to my house," I said. "And—"

But the woman was already turning away, taking Donald by the hand. "Mom!" he cried.

"I'll take care of Barney," I called to him, grabbing Barney's collar. "You go with your mom. Don't worry. Everything will be fine." I hoped I was right. The firefighters were attacking the Leonard's fire with everything they had, but to my inexperienced eye, it looked as if the structure was going to be lost. And the nearby houses?

I took a deep breath and coughed. The smoke was getting worse.

"Come on, guys," I said, unhooking the two little dogs. With no little difficulty, I led the three of them away and turned on Beale Street, hurrying as I saw two more people run past, heading for the pandemonium on Main Street. The Dalmatian didn't want to come with me and kept turning around. Without a leash, I was at risk of losing hold of his collar.

But finally, we reached my little house. I let myself inside and spoke some reassuring words to Rowdy, who got to his feet when he saw the strange dogs. “It’s all right,” I murmured to him. “You’re still my main man. We’ve just got a couple of visitors.” I put the three dogs in the kitchen and gated it off, filled a bowl with water, put down some sleeping rugs and hung the two extra leashes by the front door.

The two little dogs were cuties. Some sort of poodle mixes, one black and one apricot, both of them around twenty-five pounds, both with anxious, frightened eyes. I hesitated about leaving them shut in with the Dalmatian, but it sounded as if they were familiar with each other, and all three of them seemed so traumatized that I hoped they would just go to sleep for a while.

I watched them for a minute, then gave Rowdy a scratch and a quick peck on the head and ran back out the front door, calling over my shoulder, “Keep an eye on them, would you my man? Tell ‘em not to fight!” Unfortunately, Rowdy was already heading back to his rug to sleep, so I didn’t have much confidence in his refereeing.

I shrugged and tore down the block toward Leonard’s, hoping against hope that the fire was under control and with a sad vision of the last time I’d seen Benny Leonard, standing behind his counter so happily. I turned the corner toward Main, hit a patch of ice on the sidewalk and nearly went down. As I was struggling to regain my balance, I plowed into someone standing half-concealed behind the trunk of one of the big maples that lined the street.

He grunted and turned toward me.

"I'm so sorry," I gasped. "I didn't see—" I began, but the words died in my throat.

In the soft light from the streetlamp, and with the glow from the flames consuming Leonard's lighting his furious face like a beacon, I gazed up into the eyes of Carter Burton.

Chapter Fifteen

"Oh," I said and then, "Oh," again, not at my most articulate. My heart gave an unpleasant lurch and I felt my mouth go dry. Why had he been hiding behind that tree? *Had* he been hiding?

Bob and Madeline's son stared down at me, eyebrows furrowed and the corners of his mouth turned down in as angry a frown as I had almost ever seen.

"I'm terribly sorry," I gasped. "I hope I didn't hurt you?" I added, although with a touch of sourness. After all, I was the one who had nearly fallen. Carter Burton was the one hiding. Who was at fault here?

"... blankets!" I heard someone call, and to my relief three Burtonvillians came rushing up the street, carrying armloads of quilts.

And since Carter was maintaining a sullen silence and I wasn't, in fact, hurt—although I much feared I was about to be if I didn't get away from this stony-faced man—I scurried after my neighbors, grateful for their busy presence. My encounter with

Carter had felt vaguely threatening, and I couldn't stop my tumbling thoughts. *What was he doing hiding there? And why is he back in town? Benny Leonard had said Carter and his parents weren't on speaking terms, so...*

I threw one quick glance over my shoulder as I ran toward Leonard's, but his figure was lost in the shadows or else he had gone on down the street. I couldn't tell.

In moments, I had reached the corner, and I looked around for Ashley, but there was no sign of her. I made my way toward the other home—again with a long line of people out front sending furniture hand over hand to another home farther down the street.

A man stood, arms akimbo, watching the frantic activity. I remembered seeing him at the next table at the church, but if we'd been introduced I couldn't recall. "It's going to be okay," he murmured. "It's still burning, but they've got it contained."

I turned to look at Leonard's. There were multiple streams of water shooting at the structure, and a line of volunteers shouting at people to keep back, but the fire did appear to be slightly less fierce. I wondered if they would be able to save anything.

"Does anyone have any idea how it started?" I asked.

He shook his head. "Went up like a torch, though. One minute, nothing, next minute...all that." He nodded at the blaze. "I'd guess folks can stop moving things out of those other houses. Don't think it's going to spread."

"Lots of snow on the roofs," I commented. "Hopefully that will stop any sparks."

"Yep."

I glanced around again for Ashley, and again didn't see her, so I headed back toward the home where Barney and his friends lived, hoping to reassure the family their dogs were safe. And again, I ran right into someone, although it wasn't a collision like the one with Carter Burton. This time, I nearly tripped over a figure partially hidden in the bushes, and I stopped, a spear of anger shooting through me. Nancy Brock, of course.

"What are you doing out here?" I snapped, which wasn't a particularly fair question since most of the town was out in the streets, standing on sidewalks or helping move furniture out of homes in the path of the fire.

She sniffed and didn't answer, looking past me. I noticed she was holding a container—a bucket or a jug. I wondered what it held, but stopped short of asking. Really, there were limits to how much interrogating I could do, no matter how tempting it was.

Like Carter, Nancy wasn't talking, so without a farewell, I continued down the street, thinking evilly, *All the perps are out tonight*. I glanced over my shoulder, but Nancy had vanished into the shadows.

I found Donald and his mom, whose name was Anna Larsen. She had tears running down her face, but was looking much more cheerful. Donald ran up to me. "Barney's okay?"

"Barney's okay," I assured him. "He and his buddies are in my kitchen having a nice break from all the excitement and the smoke." At least I hoped they were resting. I didn't fancy another home improvement project if I had to replace all my cupboards after a Dalmatian encounter.

"I'll keep them overnight, shall I?" I asked Anna. "Return them to you tomorrow once things are a little calmer?"

"Barney eats at 9:00 in the morning," Donald protested.

"Then I'll get him home before nine. Better not make him miss his breakfast." I smiled. "Anything else I can do to help?"

"I don't think so," said Anna. "We'll wait until tomorrow to return everything to the house. Smoke, you know."

"Of course," I answered. "You have a place to stay?"

"Yes, my sister lives down the road. We'll stay with her. Thanks for keeping the dogs. Barney chases Elise's cat."

"No cats at my house," I said. "Just a big, friendly, very lazy dog."

Anna smiled and gave me a hug. "You must come over for dinner when the house is put back together," she said. "You've been so kind." I saw tears gathering in her eyes again.

"It was nothing. I hope your home doesn't have too much damage." I stood with her for a moment, but when she hurried away toward where her belongings were being stored, I turned to head for home. Partway there, I thought better of it and walked instead toward Myrtle Street. Was Bethany Probst frightened? She must have heard the sirens, and the fire wasn't far from her apartment. It was late, but perhaps her lights would be on and I could go up and reassure her.

I rounded the corner and peered up at her apartment. No lights. I imagined her lying in bed, sleeping soundly, although it was difficult to believe with the bedlam a block away on Main Street. But her landlord's lights were out as well. Perhaps he had bestirred himself to check on his tenant to ensure she was all right, and then both had gone to bed.

I stood in the street, the cold beginning to permeate my boots and my thick coat. I had hardly noticed it with the excitement of the fire. Then I looked more closely and started forward in horror.

At the top of Bethany's long, steep stairs to her apartment, a figure sat. Gasping, I grasped the slippery railing and tore up the icy steps, swearing under my breath. At the top, Bethany Probst sat—shivering and sobbing.

I put my arms around her, alarmed. "What are you doing out here?" I exclaimed. "Can't you get inside?"

"The lock stuck," she said, and dropped her face in her hands. "The fire...awful!"

"It's all over," I said. "The fire will be out soon. Let's get you inside. Where is your key?"

She pointed at the door and I stepped past her, grabbing the key and turning it hard. The door opened, but not without some kicking and pushing. "It isn't the lock," I said. "You've got ice built up along this threshold." *Damn* her landlord. Shouldn't it be his responsibility to make sure she was safe? This wasn't the place for her to be living, especially during a cold winter like this one.

I helped her up and put my arm around her waist. "We're going to get you wrapped in some blankets, and then I'll call 9-1-1."

"No!" she exclaimed, startling me.

I stared at her. "You should have someone check you over, Bethany," I said. "You've been out in the cold, and you're shivering all over."

"No!" she said again. "A cup of tea will fix me right up. Just get me a blanket and then you can go."

I helped her to her couch, struggled out of my coat, and threw it over her. "Are you sure..." I tried once more, but again she vehemently resisted.

"If you would turn on my tea kettle, that's all I need."

I gazed at her stubbornly, but when she looked up at me, a spark of anger in her eyes, I gave up and went into her tiny kitchen. I turned on the stove and set the kettle on, then spied a Mason jar of teabags and pulled one out.

"Is any kind of tea okay?" I called.

"Yes, dear," she answered. The old Bethany back. My mom—my grandmother. *Yes, dear.* I could hear them saying it. I gave myself a mental shake.

Soon the kettle was whistling and I poured hot water over the tea bag and carried a mug out to her where she sat on the couch. I was relieved to see that she had stopped shivering, but still she folded her hands around the mug with a grateful sigh and gave me a little smile. "The warmth feels good."

"I guess so!" I exclaimed. "I'm glad I found you when I did. How long were you out there?"

"I'm not sure," Bethany Probst shook her head and raised one hand to her brow, looking distracted and confused. I watched her in concern. "The fire ..." she said.

"It's contained," I said. "The Leonard's building doesn't look as if it survived, but the houses next door are okay. Maybe just a little smoke damage."

She sighed and looked down at her lap, clutching her tea mug. I saw a tear fall onto her hands. The silence lengthened.

"What can I do for you?" I finally asked. "Can I help you get into night things?"

At that, she looked up at me and gave a small smile. "No, dear. I can do it. I'm accustomed to sitting up late. I'll just finish this tea and then I'll be fine."

I was relieved to hear her voice was steady and reasonable. Weariness was beginning to creep over me, and I had a sudden thought of the dogs shut in my kitchen. It was time for me to get home and make sure everyone was behaving.

"Are you sure?" I asked.

"Very sure. Would you hand me that quilt over there before you go?"

"Okay." I looked around and my eyes fell on the afghan Bethany had crocheted. The one with the stars; a star for each of her foster children. I froze. Noah. The fires. I didn't want to believe it.

Rousing, I picked up a different throw and tucked it around her, hoping she hadn't noticed—hadn't guessed where my thoughts had gone.

I was relieved when she gave me a little smile and said, "Thank you. Now you run on home. Thank you so much."

"You're welcome," I said. I gave the blanket one more tuck and then let myself outside into the cold night, pausing to kick the ice away from her doorjamb.

Perhaps I could bring some salt over. And have a word with her landlord. Really, it was just too lax on his part not to take better care. She belonged in a ground floor room.

I took a deep breath of cold air and grabbed the railing to start down the slippery stairs, when behind me I heard a sound, a soft, almost toneless keening.

It was Bethany Probst sobbing, "Noah. Noah. My beautiful boy."

Chapter Sixteen

At 8:45 AM I took Rowdy's leash and, ignoring his injured look, clipped it on Barney's collar to take him and his two little pals down the street toward their home. After the very long night we'd had, I half expected the family to be still at Anna's sister's home, but instead I spied Donald waiting on the porch. I smiled. A dog lover after my own heart.

There was tape strung on poles around Leonard's and the air was heavy with smoke, but inside Anna's house the smell was not too bad and she and her son seemed to be managing all right. Donald already had Barney's breakfast ready to go and as he led his dog away into the kitchen I smiled at Anna, who wrestled the two little ones onto the back porch where their food bowls awaited.

"I'll be rather glad when their owners get back," she panted, when the little apricot dog struggled out of her arms. "April, stop that! April and Scooter, that's these two. Hungry all the time!"

"Just like my dog," I commented, as they settled down to eat. "Never passes up a meal!"

"Thank you so much for taking them last night. I almost walked down and fetched them back to save you the trouble of coming over this morning, but I forgot which house you said you were in, and to be frank I had a little trouble getting out of bed this morning."

"Understandable," I said. "I was happy to take them. You must bring Donald over someday and meet my dog, Rowdy. I think Rowdy and Donald would get on famously."

"We'd like that." Anna smiled. "How about next weekend? I kept Donald home from school today after all the mess last night, and we don't normally go out on school nights. Plus, I've got to get my house set back to rights."

"Works for me," I said. We exchanged phone numbers, I asked if she and Ashley were acquainted—naturally, they were—and I promised to call her to make arrangements.

"Is there any information on what happened at Leonard's? How the fire started, and how much damage was done?" I asked as Anna walked with me toward the door.

"I heard that Leonard's is pretty much gone. The inside is gutted. As to how it started? I'm not sure, although I overheard one of the police officers saying it could have been deliberate. I do hope they won't accuse Benny Leonard of anything! I can't believe he would burn down his own store."

"It seems pretty unlikely," I said.

Anna nodded. "I agree. And there have been …" She glanced at the kitchen where Donald was and lowered her voice. "There have been people hanging around Burtonville that I wish weren't here, you know? I saw a man—longish blond hair, kind of tall—standing outside Leonard's looking, and I wondered what he was looking at. What was he doing staring in the window?"

Longish blond hair. Carter Burton? I wondered, feeling a chill run down my arms.

Anna shrugged. "We can just start suspecting each other of stuff, though. It was probably nothing. And maybe there was bad wiring or something in Leonard's. I feel sorry for Benny."

"Me too," I said vaguely. My brain was heading in a hundred directions and I had to make an effort to pull myself back into the conversation with Anna. "Maybe we could do a fundraiser or something," I said.

"Well, I hope the insurance kicks in," Anna exclaimed. "And I do hope they rebuild."

"Yes," I said, thinking of Burtonville without Leonard's famous pizza. "I hope they do too."

I bid farewell to Barney and Donald, encouraged Anna to call if she needed anything, and headed home. My phone buzzed in my pocket and I pulled it out. A voicemail from Brad.

When I got to the house, I gave Rowdy his breakfast, assured him that he was still very definitely my main man and no Dalmatian would ever take his place in my heart, even though I had loaned Barney Rowdy's leash. Then I brewed myself a cup of tea and phoned Brad.

He answered on the first ring. "We meet at last!" he said warmly. "I thought we were going to have to resort to leaving each other voicemails. I'm hoping this is a social call and there isn't some sort of problem?"

"Well ..." I felt myself blushing. Drat the man! How could he make the heart of a sensible woman like me begin to race just by hearing the timbre of his voice? "Some of each," I said at last, once I felt I had pummeled my heart into some semblance of control.

"Wonderful!" he said. "I'm off today. Let me take you out for lunch ... dinner ... whatever."

I laughed. "I just got back from visiting one of my neighbors whose house was close to the fire last night. I still need to shower and whatnot. Early dinner?"

"Early dinner," he said. "I'll pick you up. 4:30? Italian food suit you?"

"Okay," I said weakly. A date wasn't exactly what I'd had in mind, although it wasn't unwelcome. Sitting across the table from a gorgeous man, sipping a drink on a snowy night. Why was I hesitating? *I'm not,* I told myself firmly. *I'm not hesitating.*

We said goodbye and I clicked off, glancing at Rowdy, who was staring at me. Rowdy adored Duffy. On the other hand, he adored nearly everyone, including Brad. Was my dog looking accusing? “What?” I asked him, raising my shoulders.

Rowdy didn’t answer, of course.

I took a shower, laid out a change of clothes, threw them aside, got out a different outfit, lost my temper and put on a pair of sweatpants and a sweatshirt while I waited for a clothing epiphany.

I stared at myself in the mirror. Going for an early dinner with Brad Stanton should not make me act like a teenager on her first date. I’d talked to Brad right here in my home a couple of days ago, for Heaven’s sake. But it was different—two cold, tired and stressed people taking comfort in some hot chocolate versus a couple getting a meal together.

But I had several things to talk to Brad about, and now was not the time to get sidetracked about what meant what and what didn’t. I realized I didn’t know what restaurant we were going to, but I decided a pair of black leggings, boots and a loose sweater were always appropriate, so that’s what I chose. A mustard-colored scarf completed the ensemble, and I was satisfied.

I let Rowdy out, gave him a snack, which I hoped would cause him to forgive me everything, and sat down with my quilt square in my lap. I began working on the sidewalk, carefully sewing overlapping gray stitches and adding a small tuft of green here and there. Other than the stubborn flat tire on my car, I was pleased with how my street scene was coming along. I wondered if the others had worked any more on their projects, and began pondering another embroidery party.

I passed a pleasant hour sewing quietly in my living room, and when the doorbell rang I had run through what I wanted to say to Brad to the point that I hoped I could get my questions answered without sounding too foolish.

Brad looked charmingly wind tossed and chilly, his tall frame encased in a sheepskin coat and his dark hair curling over his collar.

"Would you like to come in?" I asked.

"Car's all warm," he answered. "Might as well take advantage and head out now."

"Okay," I said, pulling on my coat and gloves. I gave Rowdy a pat, and watched Brad do likewise—another fine attribute of this handsome man. He liked my dog.

"Nice nails, buddy," I heard him murmur to Rowdy, who was already drifting off to sleep, now he knew patting time was over.

I laughed. "My stepdaughter's work. She can't resist giving him a manicure."

"Very stylish." Brad grinned.

We climbed into his car and he backed it out of the driveway, turning onto Main Street and heading east toward Prairie City. "Where are we going?" I asked him.

"*La Casetta* was what I had in mind. Have you been there?"

"No," I answered, "but Italian food is always good, and I'm going to need somewhere new to go now that my favorite pizza isn't going to be available for a while. I do hope Benny Leonard rebuilds. I loved his place."

"Sounds as if he will," Brad commented. "Store needed some work anyway. His family has owned it for years. He wanted to expand the kitchen, but he'll need more employees if he does that. Always the dilemma, right?"

"Right," I answered, and plunged in, deciding not to wait for quiet time over food to ask the question that had been bothering me. "Everyone seems so sure that gang in Peoria is responsible for the fires in Burtonville, and that Bethany Probst's son, Noah, is involved, but I keep wondering … is there any chance you're on the wrong track?"

Brad glanced at me, startled.

"I mean," I went on. "Is there a chance someone else is responsible? I've noticed a couple of odd things lately, and you did ask me to be on the lookout."

"I'd like to hear about it," Brad said. "But no, I'm quite sure we're not on the wrong track. We arrested Noah. Caught him red-handed."

Chapter Seventeen

I gasped. “Arrested him? Noah?”

“Yes.” Brad furrowed his brow. “Early this morning.”

“And are you sure ...?”

“Quite sure,” Brad said. “All of the fires had a particular method attached to them. They found Noah’s fingerprints on two incendiary devices left behind at the Abbott shed fire, and the same method was used at Leonard’s.”

I sat gazing out the window, stunned. *They found Noah’s fingerprints on two incendiary devices.* My thoughts tumbled and whirled, and all the suspicions, formed and half-formed, reasonable and unreasonable, I’d been harboring over the past few days rearranged themselves. Bethany Probst. Her beautiful boy.

I almost asked Brad to turn the car around and head home. I couldn’t imagine eating a bite of anything, let alone engaging in any sort of social behavior. All I wanted to do was to go home, hug

Rowdy and cry. The silence lengthened, uncomfortable and awkward.

"Is everything all right?" Brad finally asked, his handsome face sober.

"I just …" I didn't know what to say. Finally, "I'm just surprised and saddened." Both true. I took a deep breath. "I had hoped—or wondered, is perhaps a better term …" I stumbled to a halt. No, *hoped* is correct, I told myself savagely. I had formed an idea in my head based on what I wanted to be true. Stupid, stupid, to be so dumbfounded that I could possibly have been wrong.

"Go on," Brad said gently.

"I feel like an idiot."

"Never," he said quickly, making me smile. He glanced again in my direction and relaxed a little. "What's the matter?"

I took a deep breath and began unclenching my hands, finger by finger. I managed another smile. "Tell you what," I said. "Let me unload it all on you once we get to the restaurant, okay? In the meantime, tell me about your day."

"My day?" Brad's eyes widened. "Tell you about my day?"

"Your day," I repeated. He looked so confused that I started to laugh and all at once I felt loads better. "I'm making small talk, Brad."

"Oh," he said. "Right. My day. Well, I got up at 8:00 AM, took a shower, listened to your voicemail, pounded my head on the wall for fifteen minutes that I'd missed you …"

"You did?"

"You don't believe me?"

God, he's a delight, I thought. *Witty, dedicated, shockingly good looking.* But, "No, I don't," I said.

"Anyway," he went on. "Then I phoned you and missed you, then you phoned me and we made our date, and then I had to run through a bunch of different clothes to find the right thing to wear..."

"You did?" I asked again.

"You don't believe me?" he offered the same answer.

"This time I do. I did the same thing."

"You did?" he asked, and we both burst out laughing.

"Yes, I did," I said, and with that, Brad turned the car into a little restaurant with a lighted sign in the window proclaiming themselves *OPEN*.

La Casetta was a cozy little gem with quiet music, an extensive menu, and a nice wine selection. I ordered a glass of Cabernet Sauvignon and Brad got an iced tea. "So what's all this about?" he asked.

I sighed. "Oh, many things. Burtonville has given me lots to think about lately."

He smiled. "People think small towns are free of drama, but...nope. So what have you been thinking about?"

"Mind if I pepper you with questions?"

"Not at all. I'll answer what I can."

"Okay, let's start with Carter Burton."

Brad took a sip of iced tea. "Carter. I haven't heard that name for a while."

"Well, you asked me to keep my eyes open if I saw anyone unusual, and who pops onto the scene but Carter."

Brad grunted. "Huh. Bob and Madeline's son. The Burtons are town anchors, you know. You might've guessed by the name."

I nodded.

"There've been Burtons in Burtonville forever. Probably they settled here back in the day and the town name stuck. Anyway, Bob and Madeline are hot-tempered, as you know. If they aren't spatting with each other, they're spatting with others in their family. Carter moved out as soon as he was able and went to Chicago for a while, spent a few months in jail, then moved back to Peoria. I didn't know he'd been in Burtonville."

"I saw him in Leonard's. He's kind of a sullen guy. Has a huge tattoo on his arm, or at least on his wrist and probably on his arm—I couldn't see it. He showed up again the night of the Leonard's fire."

"Okay." Brad nodded. It looked as if he might add another comment, but I rushed on.

"Then there's Nancy Brock."

"Ah, yes. The cat lady."

"You know about her?"

Brad grinned. "Very much. I've been to her apartment to remove a couple of cats. She's harmless, I believe. A lot of trouble, but harmless."

"She creeps around at night," I said stubbornly. "And I think she's got her eye on Bethany Probst's cat."

Brad frowned. "Well, that's too bad. Let me know if I need to go get her cat back."

"Okay. She's always sneaking around carrying things. And she's another person who was out and about the night of the Leonard's fire."

"Who wasn't?" Brad asked reasonably. "Or at the Abbott fire, for that matter. The whole town turned out."

"True," I said.

"I think we have our man," Brad said gently. "Noah's got a history, we've been watching him, and he made a mistake. He cut across the cornfields north of town and set everything up the night before."

I saw him, I thought. *I saw him the night of the embroidery bee.*

I didn't bother responding. There wasn't much I could say. My sadness was returning. I looked down into my wine glass.

"Any other questions?" Brad asked. I heard amusement in his voice and I looked up into his dark eyes.

"Sorry," I said.

"Not at all. Pepper away." Brad stirred his iced tea. "Going back to Nancy, she'll turn her attention to something else here pretty soon. For a while it was recycling. She'd run up and grab a plastic water bottle right out of someone's hand. To be fair, the cat thing has lasted a while, but I do think it'll move to something else."

"What is the deal with Bethany Probst?" I asked. "Nancy Brock doesn't seem to like her, and

Ashley told me there were rumors that she and her husband neglected their children?"

"That was her husband's accusation. Noah was caught up in all that. He was difficult, and Bill—that's Bethany's ex-husband—had his own agenda, we think. Noah was running wild; Bill was sowing wild oats; Bethany was under a lot of stress. We had Child Protective Services check them out, but I don't believe anything was ever found. The children were all sent to other homes, and a couple of them were old enough to live on their own—they were just hanging out with the Forrests because of the free rent, I think."

"They never visit her!" I said. "Or at least it doesn't seem as if they do. She sits up in that apartment all alone, and her landlord is lax at best. Something's going to happen."

Something's going to happen, I repeated to myself. All my angst. Brad would think I was nuts if I told him.

Brad frowned. "Near the end, things were really difficult at the Forrest place. I actually thought Bethany might have a nervous breakdown, and Bill Forrest is an idiot at best. I heard he spent quite a lot of time turning those kids away from Bethany."

"Why?" I asked.

"Just bitterness, I think. I don't know that much about what happened, but that's what I heard. His wife was very, very close to Noah, and Bill said she was at fault for not curbing his bad behavior, for not disciplining him more, and finally, for neglecting him."

"Neglect doesn't seem likely."

"It was a stretch for him to blame Bethany for Noah's anti-social tendencies, but he just got mean near the end."

"Terrible," I said. "She loved those kids so much. And now they don't talk to her? They bought Bill Forrest's garbage?"

Brad blinked and took a sip of his iced tea. "Well, I don't know this for sure. It's all rumor. Small towns, you know." He smiled. "But, I've heard Bethany drove them away, or at least told them not to contact her."

"She did?" I was appalled. "But ... but ..." *The afghan. The photographs.* "But why?" I finally asked.

Brad shrugged. "I'm afraid I don't know."

I sat for a moment, gazing into my wine glass, surprised and saddened. She had spoken so lovingly of her children. What was going through her mind? "What about the house?" I finally asked. "The one where they all lived. Who owns that?"

"Bethany," said Brad. "She got it in the divorce—lot of good it did her. It was already in bad condition, which was one of the complaints Bill had, though that's ridiculous in and of itself. He was equally responsible for the condition of the home, and it was pretty rough by the time all this went down. I think Bethany would have liked to have stayed, but she couldn't live there alone and probably shouldn't have. She won't sell, though, and the place just sits there gathering rats and who-knows-what. Someday someone's going to complain and it'll have to be torn down. But again, small towns. People aren't in a rush for that sort of thing. It's too bad, because it would probably fetch her some money. There's a considerable amount of property with it."

"I wonder why she doesn't sell it?"

Brad shrugged.

"Did Noah burn down the barn?"

"Likely, yes," Brad answered. "But nothing was ever proven, and Bethany protected him like a tiger. Even took the blame on herself. Said she'd been out in the barn with a candle. No one believed her, and that wasn't what caused the fire anyway. Too bad it burned. It was an interesting piece of architecture."

"Yeah," I said, and fell silent, staring moodily into my wine.

"Any more pepper?"

I managed a small smile. "Guess not."

"Ok, small talk then?"

"Small talk works," I said.

And Brad was a master at it. He chatted away about Prairie City, asked about our star gazing evening, talked about his Euchre exploits, asked about my life in Peoria and even about Duane.

That was how I spent the rest of my evening with the legendary Brad Stanton, sipping wine and eating Italian food in an intimate restaurant, talking about my dead husband while he watched me with his beautiful dark eyes, smiling slightly and nursing an iced tea.

And if my thoughts drifted now and again to Bethany Probst, I thought I could be forgiven. She'd had a strange and tragic life, and now her son was likely going to prison. Would that be the end of the story?

It should be, I told myself. *Time to let it go.* But hard as I tried, I just couldn't.

Chapter Eighteen

When the later dinner crowd began to arrive, we paid our bill and left in order to free up the table. Brad took us for a drive through Prairie City and out onto the two-lane that would eventually go south toward Peoria. We drove along in silence, and I watched the frozen landscape stream by the window as the heater blasted and we listened to Mendelssohn violin concertos. I discovered Brad was a violin aficionado, another thing he attributed to his Roma ancestry.

All in all it was a satisfactory and even enjoyable evening—not what I expected, given the way things started. Finally, we turned for home and he took me to the door, making sure my house was secure and Rowdy was on the alert—or as alert as he ever was, as in asleep in the kitchen—when we walked in. Brad declined a nightcap, which was unsurprising. By that time, I'd surmised he didn't drink alcohol, but he did accept a refill of coffee in his travel mug, and before he let himself back out into the cold night, he kissed me, or perhaps I kissed him, or perhaps we just kissed each other. It was hard to tell.

As kisses went, it was a very satisfactory one. Long and warm and deep, with his arms around me and my head tucked against his shoulder. We parted company with nothing more than that, but I was tempted—oh, was I tempted! I stood, my hands to my burning cheeks and my lips and body tingling, watching his taillights disappear down Beale Street, and wondering how to feel about what. It seemed fairly obvious what Brad wanted, but what did I want?

I sighed. I had much to think about, and I blame my tangle of emotions, at least in part, for how I reacted to what happened later on that evening.

I hoisted Rowdy up from his rug in the kitchen and let him outside, gave him his supper, made myself a cup of tea—my go-to when I had things to contemplate—and sat down at the kitchen table. I debated texting Ashley or Louise or Natalie or just about anyone, but decided I'd better not—or at least not until I'd settled down somewhat, and I definitely didn't feel settled down.

Was I ready for another relationship? And was Brad the one to try it with? Louise would have rolled her eyes in frustration, had she been there, which was part of the reason I decided not to contact her. She thought I was still wearing the willow for Duane, which might have been partly true, but it was partly not true either. Who needed something more when one had already had what seemed to be the ideal? What if any other relationship I had paled in comparison?

Or what if it didn't? I thumped my teacup down on the table. My mother used to tell me I needed some fresh air when I was getting myself all worked up like this. I don't suppose she meant going out for a walk when it was fifteen degrees above zero outside, but I didn't care. I had a warm coat, and if my mother thought fresh air would help, then fresh air I would have.

I hoisted Rowdy up again and put on his leash, donned coat, boots, mittens, hat and muffler to ward off the cold, and set off down the block, Rowdy padding along beside me. It was a quiet night in Burtonville, again with the Burtonvillians—those smarter than I—snugly tucked in their homes, likely watching something fun on television or enjoying their families while I stomped down the sidewalk trying to reclaim some mental peace.

I passed the burned out remains of Leonard's and wondered what Benny Leonard was doing. Would he try to rebuild? I walked on, turned the corner again, and stopped.

Someone was moving slowly along the sidewalk ahead of me, someone bundled tightly in heavy clothing and carrying a bag or box. It was too dark to see very clearly, but I didn't like how they were bending close against the bushes and the silent trees. It looked stealthy and sly. A shiver of anger shook me. Nancy Brock and her horrible cat hunting.

She hurried across Main Street and turned south down King Street, and I looked again. I decided it wasn't Nancy, after all, then decided it was, then questioned myself again. Whoever it was seemed to be trying to keep her nighttime activities a secret, and I was tired of secret nighttime activities.

Gritting my teeth, I followed. Rowdy and I crossed Main Street and started down King, but I lost sight of her on the unlighted road. I stopped and looked around. The fields began here, snow-covered and frozen lanes of bent and cut cornstalks. Ahead was the old farmhouse where Bethany Probst, then Bethany Forrest, had raised her beloved children.

Why would Nancy be out here? Surely there were no cats to be had. And what was she carrying? What if cats weren't on her mind at all?

We arrested Noah. Caught him red-handed, Brad had said. *But what if ...?*

I walked on for another hundred feet and then stopped again. Was there a light in the window at the farmhouse? Thinking I had imagined it, I looked again, my eyes watering in the cold. Just then my cell phone vibrated, and without thinking, I answered.

It was Duffy. "Hi," he said. "How are you? I've been working on my quilt square. How's yours coming?"

"Duffy, I can't talk right now."

"Sure. Why are you talking so quietly?"

"I'm outside and there's … Can I get back to you later?"

"Wait, Marianne! Where are you?"

"Duffy, I'll call you back. Something weird is going on. I'm on King Street, just south of town, but there's … someone's … I'll call you later, okay?" And I hung up.

I stuck my phone back in my pocket as it began to vibrate again, and it was still vibrating when I began hurrying on down the road. I could see someone moving around outside the farmhouse, and my anger was rising again. What was Nancy doing at Bethany's house? When I caught up to her, I was going to find out, and I didn't care how much prying I had to do. She disappeared again around the back of the house, and I sprinted up the drive, determined to catch up with her.

It was then that I caught a whiff of smoke and I skidded to a halt, giving Rowdy's leash a hard jerk. I swiveled my head right and left, trying to see where it was coming from, then turned and looked back the way I had come, wondering if someone had a trash pile burning again. Nothing. I swiveled back and spied Nancy coming toward me, but far enough away and with her head turned toward the house so that I thought she hadn't seen me.

I glanced around and saw an old car, abandoned and rusting. I wrapped Rowdy's leash around a door handle, tugged to make sure it was secure, and left him, creeping forward along the driveway in the direction Nancy had disappeared.

Reaching the house, I put my back against the wall and peeked around the corner.

She was stopped not thirty feet away, looking up toward the second floor. I gasped in shock. It wasn't Nancy Brock I had been following. It was Bethany Probst.

I left my hiding place and started toward her, calling out, but instead of answering me, she turned and ran. I reached the spot where she'd been standing just in time to see the back of her coat disappearing into a narrow side door of the house, and then she was gone again.

I hesitated for a split second to turn on my cell phone flashlight, then went through the door after her. All I could think was that she was going to endanger herself in the house that had once been her refuge, and that grief must have made her come here, alone and at night.

The inside was in shambles, drywall crumbling, graffiti on the walls that were still standing, a door hanging askew, hinges broken. There was debris everywhere and I could smell smoke again. A chill crept up my arms. I gazed around and crept further inside, peeking into rooms and calling Bethany's name, but there was no sign of her.

Outside, Rowdy began to bellow at the top of his lungs and I heard a funny, breathy burst of noise, accompanied by a bright flash. I stopped in my tracks, my heart thundering. Then, frightened, I started back the way I had come, dodging rubble and fragments of shattered glass.

The smoke smell was intensifying, and something crashed on the second floor.

"Bethany!" I screamed. "Come out! Come out! The house is on fire! Come out!" I stumbled over something, righted myself, lost hold of my cell phone and it spun crazily away from me, the light splintering off the collapsed ceiling and broken windows.

I lunged for it, grabbed it, and started toward the door again, shrieking for Bethany, the smoke making me cough and splutter.

I tripped over the doorframe and went down on one hand in the snow, just as there was a *whoosh* and a crash from behind me, and I heard the roar of flames. I turned back toward the house, horrified, and nearly went back in, but for Rowdy, who—howling and bawling—finally broke loose from his tether and came galloping toward me. I grabbed his collar, sobbing, and pulled him away from the building. Then I fumbled for my cell phone and called 9-1-1.

"Fire!" I screamed into the phone. "Fire at the old Forrest homestead. There's someone inside!"

The calm replies of the dispatcher—"Do not, do *not* go into the structure. Walk away to a safe spot and wait for the emergency vehicles to come. I have the address and I am sending personnel to help you. I'll stay on the phone. Find a safe place. Are you in a safe place? Is someone with you? Just stay where you are. Are you in a safe place?"—while I sobbed hysterically into the phone, mingled with the crackle and roar of old wood burning, burning, burning.

Chapter Nineteen

Hours or days or minutes later, I couldn't tell, I heard the wail of sirens in the distance.

I crouched next to Rowdy, my face buried in his cold fur, crying until I thought I might be sick, my cell phone clutched to my ear with the dispatcher repeating, "Emergency personnel are on their way. Are you still safe?" and me saying, "Yes, yes, yes," and coughing from the thick smoke rolling from the flaming building.

In my distress, I hardly noticed a car traveling up King Street at breakneck speed and skidding to a halt past the driveway, backing up and then turning in. Then someone—a tall man with tousled brown hair and warm, comforting hands—enfolded me in his arms. For the second time that night I had my head tucked against a male shoulder, and hands held me tightly—so tightly.

"Duffy," I wept.

"Is someone there with you?" the dispatcher said. "Ma'am, is someone there?"

"Yes," I hiccupped. Then, "Duffy, you need to move your car. There is a fire truck coming."

"Come with me," he said firmly. "Where's Rowdy's leash?"

"I don't know. He broke free. I had him tied to that old car."

"Never mind," he said, tugging me along while I, in turn, tugged Rowdy. Soon, he had me and my dog in his vehicle, Rowdy in the back and me in the front. He accelerated rapidly off the drive and out into the frozen field, choosing a spot away from the billowing smoke and clearing the way for the fire engines that were speeding up to the house.

Once the car was parked, he leaned toward me and took my face in his hands. "Are you all right?" he said. "Are you?"

"I'm all right," I gasped. Then, "Oh, Duffy. Bethany Probst is in there."

"Someone's in *there*!?" he repeated, looking horrified. He glanced at the house. The whole right side of the structure was ablaze, and I could see solid orange behind the door where I had just emerged.

"Oh, God!" I cried, and slumped forward in my seat, racked by a new storm of weeping. I felt Rowdy's warm breath on the back of my neck and I sensed Duffy reaching out to stroke him.

"Are you warm enough?" he said. "I've got the heater going full blast."

"Yes, yes. I'm fine," I managed. But I wasn't fine. I could think of nothing but Bethany and that last glimpse I'd had of her disappearing through the door. “She’s dead. She must be dead. She was in there, and then…”

Duffy patted my shoulder and I looked at my cell phone, wondering if the 9-1-1 dispatcher was still on the line, but he had signed off, fortunately. I could hear radios crackling and shouts from the firefighters, and then the scream of a Sheriff’s vehicle arriving.

“The firefighters will find her and take care of it. There’s nothing we can do, and we shouldn’t get in the way. Let me take you home,” Duffy said. “Come on.”

“I can’t leave!” I exclaimed. “I just witnessed a death. Don’t I need to…don’t I need to do something?” I wiped my face on my arm, and Duffy handed me a wadded up tissue.

“Sorry. It’s all I have, I’m afraid,” he said. “It’s not used. Just crumpled.”

“It’s okay.” I sniffed into the tissue, wiped my eyes and blew my nose.

“Will you wait here while I go see what we’re supposed to do?” Duffy said.

“Yes.”

I leaned back against the seat, my heart pounding and my head splitting. Tears continued to pour down my face, and I wiped them again and again. I took a deep breath and scratched Rowdy’s big head. Thank God I hadn’t taken him inside with me. He huffed against my fingers and I heard him give a low whine. The car was warm and comforting, and the air inside blessedly free of the awful smell of the destruction not far away. For a moment I almost felt sleepy, and I snapped up in my seat. In the distance I suddenly heard someone screaming.

I squinted out the window. I could see two people struggling, and Duffy hurrying back toward his car.

I opened the door.

"Who is that?" I called to him, but he didn't answer. "Who is that over there?" I tried again.

"Duffy!" I cried.

He opened the door on his side of the car and started to speak, but I turned away from him. I could hear a woman's ear-splitting cries and then a sound I had heard once before, on another cold evening with Duffy out under the stars. A ghostly keening, a wail traveling over the cold air, and this time I could understand words.

"Nooaahhhh!" I heard, and I knew it was Bethany Probst. "Noooaaahhhh! Nooaahhh! Nooahhhhhhh!"

Pushing the door open, I swung my legs out into the frigid air and ran toward the two figures grappling in the dark. The Sheriff's officer and a woman with gray hair straggling out from under her scarf, fighting like a madwoman against his gripping hands.

"Bethany!" I called, running up to them with Duffy hot on my heels. Bethany turned toward me.

"Why did you go in? Why?" she shrilled at me, her face contorted.

She buckled at the knees and nearly slid out of the officer's grip as she fell to the earth. I bent next to her as he grabbed for her. He pulled out his radio, calling for an ambulance, and Bethany curled up into a ball in the snow, breathing rapidly with her bare hands pressed against her face.

I reached out a hand, feeling more tears, this time of relief, flood my eyes. "I'm so glad you're all right," I said. "You scared me ..."

She batted my hand away. "What are you *doing* here?" she gritted. "Why did you follow me?"

I opened my mouth and then closed it. She had turned her head away and now had her fists over her eyes. She moaned softly. I felt Duffy touch my back and I straightened up. He slid his arm through mine.

I looked up at him. "What's going on?" I began to cry again. "She needs help."

"The ambulance will be here in a moment," said the officer gruffly. "Why don't you go home. We'll talk with you later." I knew some of Brad's colleagues in the Prairie City Sheriff's Department, but I didn't recognize this officer.

"But ..." I began.

"I gave him your contact information, address and all," said Duffy. "We can go. I'll take you." He started to urge me toward the car, but I pulled away.

"But where did she come from?" I asked the officer. "I was positive she was inside."

"One of the firefighters nearly tripped over her," he said. "She was crouched behind that old car over there."

I looked to where Rowdy had been tied, wondering how it had all unfolded. When had

Bethany left the house, and why was she here to start with?

I crouched next to her and tried to rub her shoulder, but she pulled away. "I'm so sorry about the fire," I said. I caught a glimpse of the officer and Duffy exchanging glances, but I didn't understand. "I was afraid you were in there," I said.

"Why did you go in my house?" Bethany ground out, and then, under her breath, that sad echo, "Noooaah, Noaahhhh!"

I stood, looking from the officer to Duffy and back again and wiping my eyes on Duffy's shredded tissue.

"Let's go," said Duffy. "I'll take you home."

So Duffy took Rowdy and me back to my house on Beale Street, navigating slowly down the snow-covered streets, his car heater roaring. When we arrived, he opened the car door for me and grabbed Rowdy's collar.

"I've got him," he said, and I nodded bleakly. I was physically and emotionally drained. As useless as a rag doll. I unlocked the door and Duffy guided me inside, pushing Rowdy ahead of us. "We left his leash," I said stupidly.

"I'll get you another," Duffy answered promptly, and I managed a small smile.

I shrugged out of my coat and collapsed onto the couch, listening to Rowdy in the kitchen lapping water and no doubt spreading a giant puddle across the linoleum. I looked up at Duffy through smoke-reddened eyes. "I need an aspirin."

"Where?" he said.

"Bathroom cabinet. Right side." The night's events tumbled through my head as Duffy hurried away. Following the person I thought was Nancy Brock. The farmhouse. The flames. But Nancy wasn't there.

Bethany Probst started that fire, I thought. *It was Bethany.*

Duffy came back with the aspirin bottle, a mug of water, and a wet washcloth. "Want to put this over your eyes?" he asked.

I downed three aspirin, then leaned my head back and laid the washcloth, warm and comforting, against my stinging eyes. Duffy sat down next to me and covered my hand in his.

"I'm glad I called you when I did," he said. "I was on the two-lane heading back to Peoria from Prairie City, and not far away. What were you doing out there?"

"It's a long story," I said. "And as usual, it involves me acting like a moron."

Rowdy padded in and thumped down at my feet with a grunt. I sighed. The peace of being in the home that I loved, sitting on the couch with my friend at my side and my dog at my feet, crept into my bones and my spirit, centering me at last.

"I'd like to hear the story, if you want to tell it," Duffy said gently.

"Could we just sit for right now?"

"Of course," Duffy said. "As long as you like."

A kind man. A good man, I thought. *Shit.*

Chapter Twenty

Contrary to all my expectations, I slept like the dead, and didn't awaken until nearly 10:30AM. When I staggered out to the living room, groggy and still headachy, I found five text messages awaiting me on my cell phone. Three from Natalie, in increasing levels of urgency, one from Duffy, and one from Ashley. I also had a missed call from Brad Stanton and a voicemail from Natalie demanding that I consult my doctor about the after-effects of smoke inhalation.

Yawning, I opened the door for Rowdy to go out and started the coffee pot. While it rumbled and burped, I went to get two more aspirin and sent a message to Natalie, assuring her that I was all right, and that I had much to share with her when we talked. By now, she would be at her internship, so we would speak in the evening. I wondered how she had found out about my adventures. Likely she had phoned Duffy when she couldn't reach me. I also sent a text to Ashley, promising to call her soon.

I had spied Matt at the farmhouse fire, so I was sure she had all the pertinent details, not that she needed Matt to tell her what had happened. I was confident the entire town had turned out, just like with the Abbott fire, and gossip would be flying. She would be impatient to hear my side of the story, though. Finally, I texted Duffy and said all was well, adding him to my people-to-call list.

I fed Rowdy, poured my coffee and went to the couch, sitting down with a groan. My body felt as if I'd been running a marathon. My bones ached and my muscles were tight and sore. I closed my eyes and took a deep breath, willing the aspirin to do its thing. Then I picked up my phone and called Brad Stanton.

"Marianne," he greeted me. "You doing all right this morning?"

"Yes," I answered. "More or less."

"More or less?"

"More or less, but all in all okay. Do you know how Bethany is?"

"I knew you'd ask, so I called the hospital."

"She's in the hospital?"

"Yes. They admitted her last night. She was incoherent and irrational, and had suffered some mild burns. But she's all right, or hopefully will be—physically, anyway."

I took a sip of coffee, questions churning in my mind, but unable to form anything properly. "Maybe I should go see her," I said.

"You could," answered Brad. "But I expect she's sedated. She was pretty out of control in the ambulance. I understand she has a brother in Chicago. He's been contacted and is on his way here."

"But what happened?" I blurted. "I don't understand what happened. I followed her—I thought it was someone else, but never mind that. I followed her and she was in the house and I went in after her, and then it was on fire. But Brad, I think she set it! Did she? Did she burn down her house?"

"We are pretty confident she did."

"But why? Why would she do that?"

"We think—we're pretty sure—she did it to protect Noah."

"Noah?" My brain felt muzzy and slow, like it was trying to sort through concrete. I didn't understand anything.

"You noticed she didn't seem close to any of the kids she'd raised. Apparently, Noah was the exception. They actually contacted each other pretty frequently, as it turns out. We found the records on Noah's cell phone. We think in some corner of her mind, after she found out Noah was arrested and in jail, Bethany thought we wouldn't charge him if there was a fire he clearly could not have set."

"How did you discover all this?"

"She was pretty out of her head in the ambulance—calling out to her son and asking forgiveness, rambling. The EMTs had to restrain her a couple of times."

I settled back on the couch, staring out my window at the pretty winter scene on Beale Street—

the snow-laden trees and bushes, two kids tussling and tossing snow at each other, a woman carrying a bag of groceries, a car maneuvering slowly down the icy street. Not a block away, a lonely woman had sat in a little apartment mourning her lost children. Maybe she had pushed them away as Brad suggested and later regretted it. Maybe Noah had stubbornly refused to be pushed, and in her terror that he would end up in prison she had taken an impulsive and dangerous action.

Then I thought of Natalie and her three text messages; Natalie lying on the floor in my living room snuggled up to Rowdy; Natalie's bright, "Hi Mummy!" and decided perhaps I understood Bethany's motivation better than I thought I did. Those children. The loves of her life.

"Marianne? You there?"

"Yes, I'm here."

I leaned over and rubbed Rowdy's head where it was resting against my foot. I felt as if sadness were seeping into the marrow of my bones. Bethany Probst. I had looked at her and thought of my mother, of my grandmother. I hadn't believed her son could be guilty because of that. I suspected she was isolated, but I hadn't comprehended the depth of her abandonment and her fear. It was heartbreaking.

"Would you like me to come over?" Brad asked quietly.

I hesitated and then said, "It's kind of you to offer, but no. Not right now. I think I'd like to just chill today, maybe take Rowdy for a walk, catch a nap or something."

"Okay." He sounded a little disappointed.

"Sorry," I said.

"Not at all," he answered quickly. "You take some time to kick back today. We'll catch up later. I'm sorry I wasn't there last night—unfortunate timing with my night off. Got the lowdown when I got to work this morning."

"Is Bethany going to be all right?"

"Hope so," he said.

"She won't be charged with anything?"

Brad hesitated. "Well, there were a lot of emergency vehicles there. She'll probably have to pay something to the township for all that. But it was her property and no one was injured. It could have been a lot worse. I suppose the township could charge her with not having a burn permit or something, but that seems a little unlikely."

I pressed my lips together. I would help pay for it, if needed. I could do that much. "You said her brother's coming?"

"Yes. I'm not sure how long she'll be in the hospital, but the hospital staff said he was coming to take over after-care."

"Will she come back to Burtonville?"

"Don't know. But that wouldn't be my recommendation."

I sighed. "No, I guess not. Let me know if you hear anything more, okay?"

"Will do." He clicked off and I sat staring at my phone, feeling my headache pounding in my temples. I got up to refill my coffee cup, and as I did, my cell phone buzzed. Duffy.

"Hey," I said.

"I was glad to get your text message," he said. "You feeling any aftershocks from last night?"

"Not anything serious. Just sad." I told him the story Brad had shared with me.

"That's a tragic tale," he commented. "I hope she'll be okay."

"I do, too," I said.

"You want me to come over?"

That made me smile. "No," I said, for the second time that day. "I think I'd like to just chill for a while." *Two good men,* I thought, *both ready to stand by my side.*

"Call me if you need anything?"

"Absolutely," I said.

I clicked off and leaned back against the soft cushions. *I should phone Ashley,* I thought. But somehow I didn't want to re-tell my story quite yet. There would be time, when some of the sadness had dissipated. Maybe I would invite her over for coffee and dessert. Those chocolate chip cookies of hers ...

But what I wanted right then was to go back to bed. Pressing my fingers to my temples, I went to the kitchen and set my cup in the sink, Rowdy trailing along behind me.

"You heard the word 'walk,' didn't you, my man?" I asked. "Could we do it a little later?"

When Rowdy didn't object, I started toward the bedroom, but stopped when I heard an odd sound. For a moment, my mind took me back to the night before and Bethany's desolate sobbing, and I felt gooseflesh rise on my arms. But no, this was something different.

I went to the door, opened it and looked around. Looked around again. Looked down.

There, sitting on my doorstep, was a small, particolored tortoiseshell cat. She opened her mouth in a silent *meow*, then walked past Rowdy and me, stopping only to give her black forefoot a cursory lick.

"Well," I exclaimed. "Was that you making all that noise? I was beginning to think you were a figment of someone's imagination. Do come in," I added, a bit late, since she was already in the kitchen, where I found her lapping out of Rowdy's water dish.

I pulled some leftover chicken out of the refrigerator and cut it up for her, stroking her while she purred and purred. She ate with gusto, her fluffy tail curled around her body and her little paws tucked neatly under her. When she was finished, she did a quick wash, then went out into the living room and hopped up onto the sofa, lying down on one of the cushions as if she'd always lived in my home.

Rowdy gave her empty saucer a hopeful lick.

"You may not be able to stay," I informed her. "But you're welcome here until someone comes along to claim you. How would you feel about living in Chicago?" I hoped Bethany's brother liked cats.

I yawned and looked out the window again at my friends and neighbors going about their lives. Then I put my hand on Rowdy's head and together my dog and I went to my room to rest.

I'll need some cat food, I mused. *And some kitty litter and a box. And some bowls.* My last coherent thought as I drifted off to sleep was to wonder what Natalie—the adorer of cats—would say. It wasn't hard to imagine.

Next to my bed, Rowdy was already snoring.

Epilogue

March 1st in Burtonville and no sign of spring.

We'd had a blizzard that dumped about ten inches of snow, and I had plied the snow shovel, clearing a path for Rowdy to go out in his back yard. A drift about three feet high that I had no interest in shoveling formed against my basement door, so I made a haphazard trail around it and out into Rowdy's enclosure, turning my yard into a snow maze. It was an intriguing sight and sent me off on an Internet search of garden mazes for the summer plantings I planned to do.

Poor Ashley. She had her hands full with me and my garden dreaming. But I comforted myself with the fact that I'd helped her with her wallpapering, and she now had her eye on a large new built-in bookcase for her study. I promised to pitch in on that.

Adele, our new companion, was not deterred by the weather and—despite my entreaties—did whatever cats do outside, sometimes disappearing for several days at a time. She was a free spirit, I discovered, and there was no point in trying to dissuade her. If you attempted to keep her inside on an *I'm-going-out* day, she simply darted between your feet as soon as the door opened more than six inches. Similarly, if it was an *I'm-inside-today* day, nothing could rouse her from the couch, even the beautiful thaw that we had in mid-February.

I spied Nancy Brock skulking along the sidewalk one day, looking cat-hungry. Grabbing my jacket, I accosted her before she got close to my house, informing her that Adele belonged in my home for now and not to consider nabbing her. That was the end of my Nancy sightings, at least along Beale Street.

It wasn't clear how long Adele would be with us. Bethany Probst, it seemed, was more ill than I had imagined—both in mind and in body. She stayed in the hospital in Peoria for several weeks, first recovering from her breakdown at the farmhouse the night of the fire and then developing pneumonia.

I went to visit her one day, but I wasn't certain she recognized me, much to my sorrow. It was a relief to know her brother, Tony, seemed determined to help her. When she was released he took her back with him to Chicago. I told him about Adele, but he didn't show much interest, and Bethany did not ask after her, though I had hopes that once Bethany healed perhaps some of those memories would return. She had retreated into some private place, and said little, seeming to enjoy simply staring out the window. It made me sad to think about her, and I sent all the good energy I could muster toward Chicago.

Her landlord in Burtonville, about whom I had nurtured some evil thoughts, was growing on me. He held her apartment open in case she wanted to return, though I hoped she could find a first floor place if she ever did come back to Burtonville.

I was in my kitchen, making lava cake for my good friends who were showing up that day for a quilt square revealing party, when my phone rang. Brad Stanton.

"Hey, Brad."

"Marianne. How are you?"

"Good. About to go out and shovel my walk again. What's up?"

"Just had a bit of news I thought I'd share. It sounds as if Noah'll be going to prison for a while. He's now linked to several other fires besides the ones in Burtonville, and he'll be charged accordingly."

"Yeah. I was following the story some. How do they link someone to a fire, anyway?"

Brad chuckled. "Several ways. Fingerprints, DNA evidence, someone rats on the perpetrator, similar method of starting the fire, etc. It's complicated, but they can do it. There's an interesting fact here, though. Noah's way of lighting the fires was to attach a cigarette to a box of matches wrapped in an ignitable substance—a wad of cotton or paper and some sort of a propellant, like gasoline. The cigarette acts like a wick; it burns down and the matches light, that lights the burnables, and so on. Those are the materials we found at Leonard's, and in Noah's car. I won't go into any more details than that, since there's a trial pending. It's a pretty common method for arsonists. Low tech, but it works."

"Ugh," I said.

"And here's the interesting part. Bethany Probst was the only person on her property—other than you—the night the farmhouse burned down. But as we've pieced together the evidence from the fire, it appears it was started in a similar way to what I described above. Again, I won't go into the details, but it's odd."

"Surely they aren't trying to link Bethany to the Peoria fires or the other fires in Burtonville!" I protested, sitting down with a thump in one of my kitchen chairs.

"No, I don't think so. But it's strange, and rather sobering," said Brad. "And that barn that burned on the Forrest property so many years ago? Same method, as best we can tell."

I put my hand on my forehead. "Don't tell me any more, Brad," I said. "Bethany is an old, sick lady, and Noah's going to prison. Surely that's enough?"

"Okay, I'll stop," he answered. "But just one more thing that's going through my mind. Who taught whom?"

"Yeah," I said, a queasy shudder rolling through my stomach. "But no one's pursuing it, right?"

"No, no one is," Brad answered. There was a long pause while I hunched at my kitchen table. "Marianne?" he finally said. "You okay?"

"Yes, I'm okay. But let's talk about something else."

"Actually, I need to go in a minute anyhow. Want to grab a bite later? *La Casetta* is calling my name."

"Not tonight, but later in the week?"

"Sure. I'll give you a call."

We hung up and I sat gazing out into the living room. In the distance, I could see a pickup truck creeping by carrying lumber. Benny Leonard was rebuilding; expanding and growing his father's old store. Soon, there would be hamburgers again for Rowdy, and pizza for me, along with my favorite pastries. By spring, things would be more back to normal in Burtonville. And the Abbott place might have some new owners.

Leila Hartin had put the old house back on the market after the fires and Rose's bad spell. So, apparently, she wouldn't bring her mom back to Burtonville after all. Unfortunate, but not surprising. A lot had happened since they bought the home. The moving truck left shortly after the Abbott shed burned down.

Bethany. How was she faring, up there in Chicago? I wondered if I might look up her brother, Tony, and give them a call.

My tumbling thoughts were interrupted by three things. Adele at the door yowling to be let in, my oven timer yowling that it was time to take the lava cake out, and the glad cries of Natalie and Louise, who had met each other in the driveway and were exchanging hugs.

I took out the lava cake and shut off the oven, then turned to see Natalie entering the living room, her arms full of tortoiseshell cat. Adele was purring loudly. "Mummy!" she called. "We're here!"

I gave her a kiss on the cheek, relieved Louise of her salad, and turned to greet Ashley, who was coming up the walk carrying a tray of cold cuts and cheese. "Watch out for the ice!" I called to her and then waved as I saw Duffy's car rolling up Beale Street.

Soon we were assembled in my living room, food and drink were distributed, animals were offered their own nibbles, and it was time to unveil the quilt squares we had been laboring over as winter dragged on.

First, Louise showed her water tower, gray above a green froth of plants and flowers, and with *Burtonville* carefully stitched across the front.

Then Natalie displayed her block of the old bakery, gone now, and in its place a small antique shop.

I held up my square of the street scene, replete with the old car and its unruly tire, and Ashley presented her window box square, beautifully embroidered with a riot of different flowers.

Finally, it was Duffy's turn, but he hesitated, holding his square face down in his lap.

"C'mon, Duffy. Show it!" Natalie urged him, flapping her own square in his direction. "That's what we're all here for ... to show off our quilt blocks."

"Last time you guys made fun of me," he said grumpily.

"We weren't making fun. We were marveling at your prowess," I said. "You gotta show it, Duffy. We all showed ours."

"Yes! Show it!" added Louise, and soon the four of us were laughing and chanting, "Show it! Show it! Show it!" and Duffy's face turned scarlet.

"Okay," he called above the tumult. "I'm showing it!" And he held up his block. The room fell silent.

The old hexagonal Forrest barn, burned, the remains torn down and hauled away, was beautifully captured with Duffy's remarkable needlework. He had stitched a tree in back, so carefully wrought that one could almost hear the leaves rustling. The door to the old farmhouse, also burned now, peeked in from one corner. Behind it all, lush fields stretched away in the distance. There was a collective intake of breath and then a chorus of *Oohs* and *Ahhs.*

Duffy caught my eye and I smiled. "Let me look closer."

He set the piece of cloth in my hands and I gazed down at it, cocking my head. Above the barn, Duffy had worked stars into the midnight blue sky, and a sliver of moon rising off in the distance, like the early light in a soft summer evening. I looked up at him. I recalled telling him about my visit to Bethany's apartment and about the afghan she had worked, a star for each of her children. I felt a few tears gather in my eyes. I had looked at Bethany and thought of the family I no longer had, just as she had grieved for her children.

Then I looked around the room at my friends and my stepdaughter laughing and teasing each other, at my big black dog sprawled on the rug, at Adele in the window looking out, and I thought, *Here is my family, gathered in this room.*

Yes, I would call Bethany and ask after her, but in the meantime, there was good food and wine, and lava cake awaiting us at the end of our party. Outside, dark began to creep in, the streetlights came on and the Burtonvillians would be settled in for the evening.

I knew that soon a dazzling array of stars would spread across the cold night sky over my little town, but I could look at them another time.

About the Author

Loraine J. Hudson lives and writes in a small town in Michigan. She loves oldies rock music, stained glass, digging in her garden, playing with her dogs, horseback riding and, of course, writing. She is often at her most creative when she is taking her ex-racehorse out for an amble through the woods.

Using her pen name, Judith Wade, she has created a series of middle grades/YA chapter books that incorporate a little bit of fantasy and adventure.

Visit her at:

http://facebook.com/authorlorainehudson and http://amazon.com/author/lorainehudson